LIVING

LOSING

LISBON

AN ANTHOLOGY OF SHORT STORIES

BY WRITERS FROM AROUND THE WORLD

Hadar Badt, Jen Nafziger, Jürgen Schöneich, Kate Tyte, Marianne Rogoff, Marina Pacheco, Nadia Lym, Nuno Neves, Phil Town

Copyright © 2021 Hadar Badt, Jen Nafziger, Jürgen Schöneich, Kate Tyte, Marianne Rogoff, Marina Pacheco, Nadia Lym, Nuno Neves, Phil Town

All rights reserved.

ISBN-13: 978-1-913672-26-3

Contents

Tram 28	1
Fibrous, Local, and Nutritious	13
I'm Not a Writer but I Play One in Lisboa	23
Novena for St Anthony	40
Alive in Lisbon	48
White Rabbit of Lisbon	60
Iberian Summer Cruise	79
Lisbon Blues	88
Dream Destination	97
O Senhor do Adeus	101

Welcome to the Living, Loving, Longing, Wonderful World of Lisbon

Welcome to this anthology of short stories set in Lisbon. I've lived in Lisbon twice, for four years in the '90s and I'm now entering the third year of my return. In between, I visited regularly. So you could say I have an ongoing love affair with the city.

Over that time, Lisbon's outward appearance has hardly changed. It's a beautiful city with glorious light that attracts tourists and artists alike. Technology, though, has changed the way people work, live, and play, as much in Lisbon as everywhere else.

It was technology that drove the Lisbon Writing group online during the Covid lockdown. Until then, our lovely hosts used to organise in person meetings. Because the group was on Meetup, many travelling writers dropped in on those in-person meetings when they were visiting the city.

When the meetings went online due to Covid restrictions, the regular locals were joined, and often rejoined, by travellers who could once again connect with fellow writers through the magic of the internet.

Over the last nearly two years, I have loved meeting the wide diversity of writers of all backgrounds, countries, ages, languages, and levels of ability. There is something special about hanging out with people who want to create.

We all learn so much from each other. We've shared poems and short stories, extracts from novels and biographies, and a stunning variety of creative works generated by writing prompts. It was my fascination with the way people could all start with the same prompt and produce such wildly different tales that inspired this anthology. We took a city we all know and love as our starting point and then wrote whatever we wanted.

I'm thrilled with the result. I hope readers will enjoy these short tales that shine a disco ball of wildly different lights on Lisbon.

Marina Pacheco
Lisbon 7th October 2021

Tram 28

Hadar Badt

Nope, I wasn't having any fun. I stared at the gloomy world outside and inhaled the scent of rain and dust through the slightly open window. The famous 28 tram was packed with people, and there was not enough air to go round. I brought my face closer to the narrow crack of air, the raindrops that splashed inside mixing with my silent tears. We had just passed the iconic Lisbon Cathedral, but I couldn't have cared less. Not because I wasn't impressed by the 13th century Romanesque-style building with its two clock towers, but because I was dumped by my boyfriend on WhatsApp right before exiting Lisbon's airport two days ago.

I was about to walk through the sliding glass door when I heard an incoming message. After several hours with no Internet connection, I couldn't resist the urge to check my phone. It was probably Adam checking up on me and verifying I'd arrived safely in Lisbon. I smiled to myself when I thought of him. Although we were only five months together, it felt like we had known each other our entire lives. I had a good feeling about him. He couldn't join me on my Portugal getaway because of work and urged me to take the trip on my own. I remember thinking how lucky I was to have such a considerate boyfriend. He knew just how much I needed time off after a stressful year. I put the luggage aside and rummaged through my handbag, fishing for my phone. The minute I opened Adam's message, I heard a deafening thunder. It was so strong that I nearly lost my grip on the phone. The message read:

"I can't do this, Daphne; I can't do us. I'm sorry, but I'm not ready like I had thought. I hope you'll still enjoy your vacation. You deserve to be happy."

Just like that, the heavens opened and poured down all the misery they had been storing above in the most biblical of ways. I stood speechless at the entrance, ignoring polite requests to move aside from the passengers who were walking inside with their cumbersome luggage.

The rain intensified, knocking violently against the glass walls. What in my mind was supposed to be a sunny vacation turned into a rainy disaster, and it wasn't because of the unexpected rain. I don't know how long I just stood there, refusing to acknowledge what had just happened. I felt a hand or two tapping my shoulders and concerned voices asking me if I was okay. I couldn't form words and I might have nodded, as I saw their blurry figures walking away from the corner of my eye.

An elderly couple sat in front of me. The man caressed the woman's neck as they exchanged their impressions of the moving scenery. I bit my trembling lips, trying to prevent my sorrow from manifesting itself as a scream or miserable sob. *That* kind of love was a relic of a world long gone, a world to which I didn't belong. Mine was an Instagram world that only delivered virtual love in the form of likes, emojis, and one too many filters. In my world, people didn't grow old together but rather grew tired of each other or simply moved on to the next fresh conquest. I was sure that Adam and I were meant to be, and now he was just another ghost from my past.

The tram rattled and screeched as it made its way along the black cobblestones. I clenched my fists and tried to ignore the long ponytail that swooshed into my face with every twist and turn. The long ponytail belonged to a brunette teenage girl. Her parents sat right behind us, imploring her to pay attention to Lisbon's landmarks through the rain-dotted window. It's a pity to miss out on Lisbon's most famous tour after standing in the queue for nearly an hour, they reminded her. The girl preferred to ignore them, moving her head to Britney Spears' "It's Britney Bitch" song AKA "Gimme More." *Someone needs to tell her 2007 is long gone....* She was wearing childish pink headphones with matching cat ears. The music was so loud, I could hear everything.

I was also one of the idiots who stood in the long queue, waiting for my turn to go on a ride that was a must according to every Lisbon travel guide. While the others took refuge under umbrellas, I tested the resistance capabilities of the blue rain poncho I had bought in Peru seven years ago. Surprisingly, despite all the time that had gone by, the poncho passed the test with flying colors. I wasn't particularly excited about falling willingly into this tourist trap from hell, but it was better than staying all day long in my Airbnb room and crying.

The tram squealed before stopping at the next station: Basílica da Estrela, an 18th century Baroque monument which was built after Queen Maria gave birth. Her son, Jose, was an heir to the Portuguese throne. Sadly, he didn't live long enough to see his mother's gift for him; he died of smallpox two years before the construction of the Basílica was completed. Talk about irony. I looked at the marvelous façade, wishing I could have had some of my fellow passengers' zest in my tired eyes. I cried for two nights in a row and there wasn't really any point to this vacation, but I was worn out and wasn't quite ready to go back to the office. The teenage girl with the annoying ponytail got up from her seat after her parents called her name at least ten times. So, she was a Tiffany. The girl frowned and followed her parents out of the tram. Not wanting to form any kind of connection or, God forbid, chit-chat, I glued my eyes to the window, staring blankly at the Basilica. I heard my new bench neighbor sitting down beside me. I couldn't tell if it was a man or a woman, but it sounded like that person was wearing a plastic cover of some sort. I didn't have any plan in mind. I could either stay on the tram all day long or get off somewhere and find something to eat. It was a quarter past one in the afternoon and my stomach started growling. Seeing that I felt like an empty zombie for the last two days, I was surprised that I still had my appetite.

The sky was colored in a dark gray, smothered by thick rain clouds that refused to let any ray of sun make its way down to us. So much for trusting the weather forecast… All the doors closed, and the tram resumed with its jangly ride. I minded my own business, chained to my poisonous thoughts, when my new tram-neighbor asked: "Excuse me? Do you speak English?"

I pretended not to hear him and continued running a million different scenarios in my head, trying to understand what I had done wrong with Adam. Obviously, I knew that wallowing in my misery would bring me nowhere, but I couldn't help it.

The man cleared his throat and tried again. "Are you okay?"

What was wrong with him? Couldn't he see that I wasn't in the mood to talk? I nodded, hoping he would leave me alone.

"It's just that, um, well—ah, what I mean to say is—"

"What?!" I snapped at him and half-turned only to realize that the man who was looking at me with brown apologetic eyes was damn cute, with his two dimples and his gorgeous shoulder-length brunette hair. He didn't sound like a native English speaker, but I couldn't quite place his accent.

"You're crying," he said and lowered his gaze.

"I'm not crying, these are raindrops." I gestured at my face, then at the open window. I wiped away the so-called raindrops from my face.

"Okay," he said, without looking at me.

He probably thought I was the biggest monster in the world. I felt guilty for lashing out at him and added, "I appreciate your concern, though."

The man nodded without making eye contact. I couldn't blame him. Like many other people who didn't know me, he had expected me to act the way I looked: I had the girl-next-door kind of look, meaning people assumed I was polite and flower-gentle. This was mostly true when I was in a good mood. But when I was angry, all hell broke loose. If there was ever a competition for Portugal's shittiest tourist, I would surely win first place. People were so friendly with me here, but I either ignored their offers to help me or, even worse, demanded from them to leave me alone and mind their business. Who knew that Portuguese were the Canadians of Europe?

"I'm sorry," I said under my breath. "I'm having a bad day."

"Clearly," he said.

"I'm not as scary as you might think." I wrapped a group of curls around my finger, one of my many bad habits when I wasn't at ease.

The man grinned. "You could have fooled me," he smirked and touched his hair. It was still wet from the rain. "So, how do you like Lisbon so far?"

"It's been raining for two days straight. Yesterday I spent all day long in a mall, watching five different movies. One of them was *Pokemon: Detective Pikachu.*"

The man chuckled. The people who sat behind us were clearly eavesdropping on us, as I heard their suppressed laugh.

"In my defense, I can say that I had intended on only watching *The Joker,* but the movie made me want to scream and I needed to counter its disturbing effect. It's because of the stupid rain."

"It's just bad luck. You came to Lisbon on the rainiest week of the year." He smiled and shook his head.

"I'm all about bad luck this week," I mumbled, the image of Adam's awful message still lingering in my head. "What is it? Why the headshake?"

"You're funny."

"No, I'm miserable, there's a difference." We both laughed. I felt the tension of the past days leave my body. "I'm Daphne," I said, trying to counter my bitchiness a bit.

"I'm Miguel. Where are you from?" he asked.

"You first," I teased. I wasn't a big fan of this question, mostly because the minute you expose your nationality, people assume things about your character without even knowing you.

"I'm from here." He was wearing a red raincoat that looked too small for this wide chest and broad shoulders. Did he put it in the dryer and caused it to shrink? Why was I thinking about his raincoat? Was I that desperate to take my mind off things? "Your turn," he said.

"I'm from all over the place. My parents moved around a lot when I was growing up."

"I never had the chance to live elsewhere." Miguel lowered his head, as if he was ashamed of this fact.

"Trust me, I would have preferred to stay in one place for a change, but we didn't have much choice because of my parents' jobs." Traveling was my default mode. Staying in one place was the exception. How stupid was I to think Adam would be the reason I'd finally take roots and stop moving?

"You must have seen the entire world by now," he said, a hint of jealousy in his eyes.

"Not quite. It's not a small world, after all." I grinned as the melody of that boat ride in Disneyland played in my head. "I've never been to Lisbon before."

"And what brings you here?"

A bump along the way made our heads bang against one another. "Are you okay?" I asked. I put my hand on top of the aching part of my head and laughed. I didn't even know why I was laughing.

"You have some head!" Miguel chuckled. "I'll survive. So, about my question. ..."

"Probably the same thing that brings a Lisbonian to go on tram 28, cramped with annoying tourists." The two fancy-dressed women who were sitting on the other side of the aisle glared at me, nearly killing me with their eyes. I cleared my throat and added, "annoying tourists like *me*."

Miguel laughed. "I doubt it."

"And why is that?"

"I woke up in a grim mood today," he said.

That took me by surprise. He seemed so perky to me. It goes to show how clueless we are when it comes to someone's inner world. Outside, he could smile and look happy when he's fighting a bloody, ugly war inside. "Is it because of the rain?" I asked.

"No. I woke up feeling empty. I've been living in auto mode for far too long. Each day seemed the same. I needed a change, something to happen, anything."

"Yeah, the routine can kill you slowly."

"I didn't feel like going to work, so I took the day off."

"And you decided to wander around in the rain?"

"Yes. I know most people dislike it, but I always feel better after walking in the rain. It's such a reviving feeling. It's almost like I'm a new person after that."

"And the tram?"

"I was walking near the station when the tram pulled in. I didn't have anything better to do, so I climbed up." Miguel shrugged. The fabric of his raincoat stretched around his shoulders to the point of nearly bursting. "Now you," he said.

While I was deliberating whether I should tell him about the breakup, the tram stopped. The other passengers got up from their seats and looked like human sardines as they made their way out of it.

"That's it?" I was hoping the ride would be longer, so our conversation wouldn't have to end.

"Yes, it's the last stop. Let's go." Miguel stood up and gestured with his head for me to follow. We both wore our hoods, ready to face the raging rain.

"Where are we?" I asked when we were both outside.

"Prazeres cemetery. Come on, let's go." We walked to the fancy entrance made of two marble poles with a big cross on top. I remembered reading about this cemetery before my trip. It was the biggest cemetery in Lisbon and considered one of the most beautiful cemeteries in the world. I had no intentions of visiting it, though, as cemeteries gave me the chills.

A spacious plaza awaited us, separated by white mausoleums on both sides. We crossed the plaza and turned left just before reaching the church, then chose a path with tall Mediterranean cypresses. It felt like we were in a maze of mausoleums and trees, and no matter how much we'd walk, we'd never get to the other side. The downpour was replaced by a gentle drizzle. We saw a guided group in the distance. The tourists were hidden under their umbrellas, nodding as the tour guide explained things I couldn't hear.

"It's your turn," Miguel said.

"My turn?"

"To tell what brought you to Lisbon."

"Oh. Someone I know told me how wonderful Lisbon is. That's why I'm here." I sighed. About a month ago, while Adam and I were having a late breakfast on a lazy Saturday, he said that we should visit Lisbon together some time. He couldn't stop praising it. That he didn't want to join me in the end should have raised a red flag.

"I'm assuming someone who's close to you. Perhaps a man?" Miguel asked.

"How did you know?"

"I have three sisters. I know that look you have when a certain man pisses you off." He grinned goofily and his cheeks slightly reddened.

We both grew quiet. It was one of those tension-filled silences that appeared awkward, but was actually an anticipation-silence, letting both sides know that something out-of-the-ordinary was about to happen. We continued walking without saying a word for a while, silly smiles spread across our faces.

"Are you hungry?" Miguel asked.

Oh no. He must have heard my stomach. "Just a bit." I laughed awkwardly. Of course, I lied. I was famished.

"Our stomachs all speak the same language, regardless of where we're from," Miguel said and gave me a friendly nudge. "Do you want to get out of here and grab something to eat?"

"Sure."

As we made our way to the entrance of the cemetery, the rain gradually stopped. Delicate rays of sun pierced the sky and cast their light on the trees. A small sparrow stood next to a puddle and drank water.

"Look!" Miguel exclaimed.

A perfect rainbow appeared above our heads. I sighed in relief. Maybe this vacation wasn't a complete disaster. I glimpsed at Miguel, who nodded to himself, as if he could read my mind. It was time to leave the dead and let them rest in peace; it was time to start having some fun.

Hadar Badt

Hadar is currently residing in the fun-loving hipster paradise of the Middle East, AKA Tel Aviv. When she's not busy working or volunteering with four-legged friends, she writes goofy comedies, short stories, and flash fiction in Hebrew and English.

She lived in four countries on four continents, and she speaks four languages. She might have a thing with the number four.

Her debut rom-com novel *Free Falling* will be available on Amazon in a few months. Visit her website—https://hadarbadt.com—and Facebook page—https://www.facebook.com/HadarBadtWriter—to stay updated.

Fibrous, Local, and Nutritious

Jen Nafziger

Emory eyed the five-story apartment building from the safety of the taxi's window. Pushed up against a graffiti-covered, vacant building on one side and a closed, degenerate-looking bar on the other, it didn't seem like the type of place a sophisticated woman would choose to spend her time.

Then again, what did Emory really know about this woman--this Tara? They'd met only the night before when Tara, a beautiful, mysterious stranger--invited Emory over for an intimate dinner date after they met on the beach.

Now, Emory clutched his paper parcel tighter against his chest like a security blanket. Perhaps this wasn't such a good idea.

"You getting out?" The driver clucked.

Emory met the man's eyes in the mirror. He should

tell the driver to turn around. In fifteen minutes, he could be back in bed, reading a book about military history, as usual, instead of at the foot of some unknown encounter in a foreign country.

"I..." he started, but didn't finish. What exactly was he supposed to do? Why did he even come to Portugal in the first place?

It was a co-worker who first presented the travel package to Emory. A reduced-price week at an upper mid-range hotel that included airfare, breakfasts, and a premium beach chair. Sure, it was an excellent deal, but he still protested at first. Emory was not the kind of man to whisk himself away to exotic locales––no matter the discount––but the others at the accounting firm goaded him on.

You're as pale and dull as a spreadsheet these days, they said. Wound too tight. Get out from behind the books and shake things up on a beach somewhere. Bring back some stories, they told him.

Eventually he caved. At that price point, the package was just too good of a deal to pass up. The entire firm wished him well when Emory left, but what would they think of him now? Too afraid to even get out of a car?

He gulped. No. Not today. He needed at least one story to bring back to the accounting firm. It was time for Emory Billings to have an adventure.

The famed Lisbon sun faded into black overhead as Emory tucked the parcel under his arm and stepped out of the cab. No sooner had his sandaled feet touched the cobblestone street than the driver squealed away, leaving only a small snarl of hot exhaust on Emory's bare calves. The spitting heat soon dissipated into cool, night air.

The city was different after dark; it was spooky and Emory didn't like it. He forced his legs forward towards Tara's building. This was only the second time he'd been outside after sunset on his trip. The first was the previous night, when he met Tara at a full moon dance party on the beach outside his hotel.

Attending such a bacchanalian romp was wholly accidental on Emory's part. He originally strayed from his room to ask if the DJ wouldn't mind turning the music down, but soon found himself dumbstruck by an absolute vision.

She stood alone, silhouetted by party lights in a scarlet dress that appeared simultaneously flowing and body conforming. They drew each other in at once, each making their way towards the other as if by instinct. Her dark blue eyes, flecked with golden starbursts, enthralled him completely. The music was too loud for them to talk much, but she managed to communicate the dinner invitation and handed him a piece of paper with an address, a time, and her name; Tara. Delightful, alluring Tara.

Emory reached the apartment building's vestibule and stood for a moment. Tara was a deeply passionate and exciting woman. What if last night was a fluke? He was surely not the seductive man of adventure Tara was expecting.

Still, he'd come this far. It was simply a matter of pretending he was the sort of confident heartbreaker who had illicit affairs. It was only one night, after all. Emory wiped sweaty hands on the side of his stiff, new khaki shorts and reached for the intercom.

As he waited for a response, Emory studied the blue and white tiles that covered her building's facade. Repeating diamond and square shapes of some kind–– most of the tiles were like that in the city. Though, in the dim light Emory swore they looked more like open, fanged mouths.

"Hello, darling." A feminine voice finally crackled on the electric speaker's coils, startling him back to attention. "Come in. I'm on the top floor."

The door buzzed, Emory entered, and tried not to squish his parcel as he tucked himself inside the tiny, old-fashioned elevator. It felt more like an upright coffin as his droopy shoulders squished against each solid side. He slid the hinged door shut and pressed the topmost button.

When the elevator shuddered to a stop, Tara was already waiting for him, draped in a scarf and standing dramatically, one arm thrown above her head on the doorframe. Instead of scarlet, she wore a silk negligee of midnight blue, which contrasted against her skin like storm clouds against a bright moon.

"Hello, lover." She shot him a sultry look, licked her lips. "I'm getting hungry."

A red, hot ring formed around the collar of Emory's

equally red polo shirt. Why did she word it as if she were going to eat him? Emory dislodged himself from the elevator, suppressed the growing anxiety in his stomach, and shuffled towards the doorway.

As he got closer, he saw Tara narrow her eyes at his outfit then appear to shake something from her hair. Emory wondered if he'd chosen the wrong clothes. Was she expecting a nice pair of slacks instead? He didn't have long to dwell. Tara beckoned him forward with both arms. As soon as Emory was fully inside the apartment, the door slammed shut. He jumped.

"Sorry. Old building." Tara slid her hand up his arm and moved her pink lips close to his earlobe. "We won't let that ruin the feast."

Emory's heart raced. He began to shake––with fear, anticipation, or delight, the accountant did not know. He just knew that her touch was the cause. He stepped back and thrust the paper parcel out in front of his ribs as a barrier between them.

"I got bread," he said in one loud burst.

Tara took the heavy bag and looked down at it.

"From the farmer's market this morning. I met the baker. It's Artisanal rye. Very nutritious. Full of fiber."

"How nice." She winced, as if the bag contained a hive of live scorpions instead of a dense and nutritious loaf of local, organic, multi-grain bread.

"Do you not like it?" Emory asked with a tilt of his head. Had he made another mistake? What did women like on dates anyway? Perhaps he should've picked up some of that chunky, fresh sheep's cheese instead.

"Let me just... put this in the kitchen." Tara turned and disappeared around the corner.

"Just keep it airtight. You don't want mold."

There was no response.

Emory folded his hands together in front of his reversible belt and rocked on his heels. As Tara fiddled with something in the other room, he took a look around.

The apartment was quite dark. Heavy black curtains obscured every window. The only light came from dozens of flickering candles. Their minuscule flames illuminated tall, menacing sculptures in the corners and highlighted the sharp noses of strange wooden masks that hung from heavily papered walls.

"Nice place you got here." He called, as he picked up a large, sharp-edged crystal from a nearby end table. "Real cozy."

Who was this fascinating woman? And what in the world did she want with him?

A shiver crawled up Emory's neck as he set the crystal back down. This place was bizarre, frightening even. Part of him wanted to run away at once, but he stopped himself. Apprehension was expected on real adventures, wasn't it? Trying new things was good. And, who knows, maybe pitch-black rooms full of candles and scary artwork were perfectly normal for the type of people who had one-night stands.

Tara reappeared, carrying two round goblets which were filled to the brim with thick red liquid.

"Here, darling." She handed him one of the glasses. "This one is yours. Let's drink to us."

"Is this wine?" Emory sniffed at the contents as some dribbled over the side. "Can't drink it, I'm afraid. Allergic to the tannins." He sat the glass down on the table next to the crystal, hoping he wasn't offending his host too egregiously. "Got any of that Portuguese orange soda?"

Her pale, beautiful face dropped in shock. He felt the air leave his lungs. Why was he such a failure at love? Every move he made was wrong. He needed to bring her back somehow.

"... or passion fruit?" He added, as sensually as a senior-level accountant could manage. "I liked that soda flavor, too."

Tara made some sounds that Emory couldn't interpret. However, the head shaking and closed eyes communicated her message clearly.

"I'm sorry." His chin dropped to his chest. "I'll just see myself out." Emory turned and trudged towards the door, or, where he thought the door should be. It was difficult to see in the candlelight.

Bread? You idiot! He yelled at himself as he pawed for the handle. Forget someone like Tara––how would any woman ever want him? His hand finally clenched the knob. He began to turn it.

"You're not going anywhere." Tara called. She rushed

towards him, bringing with her swirls of heavy incense-scented air. Her hand dropped down on his forearm,

Emory's heart leapt to his tonsils. Was she reaching for his wallet? Was she a vampire? Or part of a scammer ring targeting lonely, middle-aged tourists? Why, oh why, did he let his colleagues talk him into this trip in the first place? He was going to get murdered in this weird apartment with this ... this ... crystal-loving sorceress!

"Look, I..." he sputtered, raising his arms to his face in self-defense. Could he strike a woman if it came down to it?

Tara ignored his flustered gasps. She reached behind him with her free hand and flipped on the light switch.

The room immediately filled with a harsh, artificial glow. Emory's eyes cringed against the glare for a moment, then adjusted. Tara, now fully illuminated, released her grip on his arm and stepped a few feet back.

She was at least ten years older than he thought. The blue dress, though once fine quality, was frayed and faded here and there, betraying a figure that wasn't quite as perfect as Emory remembered from the previous night.

"I'm sorry. I'm not good at this. And now I've disappointed you." Tara sighed.

Emory cocked his head to the side again, pulse still racing.

"It's so stupid. My mother pushed me to come here. To get out of my head." She touched her forehead, her long, graying hair. "I've been here almost a week, but everyone I've tried to approach has either been too sexy or too young or not interested in somebody like me." She gestured towards Emory with a smile. "But, when I saw you, I thought that you were so confident. Out there on the beach, dancing on your own."

Emory recalled the moment before talking to Tara. He'd tripped over a sandcastle and made several desperate stumbles to stop himself from falling. He supposed that, under a full moon, it could've looked like some kind of tantric dance.

Emory said nothing, but his heart slowly descended from his throat to its rightful place in his chest.

"That's just not me. None of it is." She motioned to the awful figurines and dangerous artwork behind them. "This isn't even my place. It's a studio that belongs to a friend of my mother."

Emory nearly laughed in relief. Was it possible that this woman was even worse at courting than he was?

"I'm actually staying at the same hotel you are. I just wanted you to think I was interesting, that I knew what men liked." She looked down and wiped a tear from her cheek. "The truth is," she exhaled in a huff from her nose, "I'm not a party person. I'm a claims adjuster."

Emory's cheeks flushed. He beheld Tara––the awkward insurance administrator. A loon who tried to seduce him of all people, who hauled him all the way out to this weird studio, even though they were staying in the same hotel. He had only one question for this woman.

"Did you get the same package deal with the premium beach chair and the breakfasts?" He asked.

"Of course." Tara scoffed as if he'd asked the world's most ridiculous question. "And my flight was delayed, so I'm filing a travel reimbursement claim."

Emory emitted a small, involuntary squeak. His heart rustled like a stack of freshly sorted documents. Dear, fascinating Tara. This magical answer to a question he didn't even understand how to ask. This story to end all stories.

"Darling." Emory stepped up to Tara. She smiled as his fingers trailed up her arms and came to rest on his shoulders. "How would you like some rye bread?"

⚓

Jen Nafziger

Jen Nafziger is an award-winning cosmic writer and poet who lives in Lisbon, Portugal. Her publishing credits include small presses, chalked-up sidewalks, bar napkins, and hastily written notes tacked to overflowing bulletin boards.

I'm Not a Writer but I Play One in Lisboa

Jürgen Schöneich

I am standing on a hill near the Universidade Nova de Lisboa. Above my head the planes are screeching on their approach to the airport. They are flying low, they know their destination, the wheels are already unfolded. Just a moment before, not even two hours ago, I was sitting in one of these mechanical birds, looking down at this hill, then at the Sete-Rios train station, the Hospital de Santa Maria, the highway, and then the plane touched the ground with a spring. I arrived, and now Lisboa enters my body, my clothes, pervades my skin, like a warm sweet rain.

⚓

There is Lisbon and there is Lisbon. All the Instagrammer

and selfie snappers of the world love this city, love the monastery, the streetcars, the egg tarts as well as all the trendy restaurants and bars, all the must-sees you can do in 48 hours. For me, that's fine. But my Lisboa is a very different city. It's like those picture-puzzles where people see different things in the same picture.

The further away you get from the city center, the older the people you see on the street. It is early morning, I am sitting in the Café Central in Almada, around me many senior citizen. It is noisy in the café, most of the old men and women know each other, they greet their friends and look forward to a day where many stories will be told. Stories from a life when they were not yet seniors, the children not yet grown up, when they were on their way to work in the morning instead of meeting friends in the café. People are sitting in their coats, the door is open, it's a cold day in December. I open my laptop and create a new document, a blank page. In the guesthouse it took me some effort to explain why I didn't want to have breakfast there, although it was included in the price of the room. But I am here on a voyage of discovery. I watch a woman in her fur coat at the next table and imagine what her life is like and what she is thinking about. She's sitting by herself in a café where hardly anyone else is alone. I imagine a younger version of this woman as she hurries purposefully through an office. It could be a scene from a movie.

I bought first my journal made by Papelaria Emílio Braga at the FNAC in the Vasco da Gama shopping center. It has a nice cover with a drawing of a streetcar and the name of the city, Lisboa. The pages are tinted slightly yellowish and on the first page you can read the history of the company, "... what would become one of the best stationary stores." A notebook like from 100 years ago, and it is now full of thoughts and ideas. Today I make my way to the small factory where these books are being manufactured. It is located very close to the airport in an industrial building. On the other side of the street they prepare the food wrapped in plastic for those passengers who will be on their way from Lisboa to somewhere else.

The small factory looks like a museum. Every step is manual labor, the men and women working here wear gray smocks. I'm sitting on a chair waiting next to stacks of notebooks. It's lunch time, the woman who sells journals to individuals isn't here yet. When she arrives, I'm greeted very politely. The six books I have bought are carefully wrapped in paper, and as a thank you for my purchase I am even given three small exercise books. Grateful, I make my way back to the bus stop, a 20-minute walk in the midday sun.

⚓

I want to write about the old train station in Barreiro, but I don't know how to express what fascinates me. It is a beautiful building, visible from afar when you are on the ferry from Lisboa. The station shines in the evening sun.

But when you step into the hall, there is a moment of shock. I feel silence here, no people, no kiosks, no loudspeakers, no screeches of brakes. No goodbyes, no welcomes, no tears, no people rushing through the hall to get the train. It's a station without tracks. A station that lost its job and now doesn't know what the future will bring. Maybe the building will be lucky and there will be someone who needs it. Maybe not. I'm standing on the platform noticing, there are still flowers in the flower pots and someone has to water them regularly. As deserted as this station looks, there is someone who takes care of it.

⚓

If you like to watch tired people, I recommend you to take the ferry to Cacilhas at 11 pm. It is quiet in the waiting room, hardly anyone speaks. As the ship moors, people gather in front of the large door that is about to open. Some passengers are impatient. If you have to catch a tram in Cacilhas, you need a seat on the ship near the exit. Buses and trains do not wait, and the way home is still far. There's a small bar onboard, where you can have the last coffee of a long day.

⚓

The Alentejo Grillhouse is purely Portuguese. The ladies behind the counter are beauties, as are many women in Portugal, but they aren't beautiful in a fashionable way, but rather in a "three kids and a lazy husband" way. The last time I asked one of the ladies if she spoke English, she said "friend" and looked toward the kitchen door.

When I eat at Alentejo Grillhouse, I order with my hands and my eyes. The whole procedure is a bit complicated. Some people order at the counter, wait for their food, and pay at the register. Or they write something on a piece of paper, pay at the register and get the food brought to the table. Today I want the steak with Portuguese sauce. I look at the photos of the different dishes they offer. With my phone I take a picture of the photo with the steak and show it to the lady behind the counter. I say the word "rice" and try to say "arroz" too, she shouts something to someone else. I believe it means my order has been taken. Then I push my tray a bit further, and the other people look at me, frowning. What did I do wrong? I can't figure it out, the Portuguese are a polite bunch, they just frown.

The cook prepares my steak, puts it on a plate, and puts it somewhere far away. I try to get his attention. He's wearing safety goggles, as if he were a welder or a man working on a construction site. He looks like a ghetto kid from where Marvila transitions into the Bronx. Now he stares at me like everyone wants to buy drugs from him, and he doesn't like it. A minute later I get my steak, rice, and salad, and that makes me feel like a real Portuguese from the Alentejo.

A magical place, the Cemetery of Pleasures, Cemetério dos Prazeres on Christmas Eve, just before the sun goes down.

It is located on a hill, I can see the city, the river and the bridge behind the graves. The cemetery looks like a small town of the dead, there are streets and small houses where they wait. Some doors are fitted with windowpanes so you can look inside. Often there are shelves for coffins, they remind me of a sleeping car compartment for a very long journey. Above the portals of the small houses there are long names that must have meant a lot to people when they were alive. But tonight there is no one here to read them except me. In some graves candles are burning. Trashcans wait by the roadside, as if orderly citizens have put them out. I look at the memorial to the firefighters who died on duty. An elaborate pile of rubble carved out of stone, beams, columns, and poles protrude from it. Skulls made of stone lie on crossed bones, very realistic. The fire department also has its own area in the cemetery, small graves, on each tombstone a photo of the deceased, serious faces, no one smiling.

It is lonely here, but not silent. Minute by minute, airplane after airplane thunders above the graves, wide-bodied aircrafts like those used for long-distance flights. Probably full of people on the way to their families, who are already setting the table for the exquisite meal on Christmas Eve. And I'm sitting here on a bench in the space between, next to me the dead in houses, above me the living in the air.

Now it is already dark, I'm walking through Campo de Ourique to Largo do Rato. Shopkeepers stand in the doorways of their small stores wearing their finest clothes.

They are talking to the owners of the stores next door. It's the moment of calm before the storm of grandchildren, kissing, talking, and celebrating will start, the grand feast that supermarkets and alcohol companies advertise on television before, a day later, the manufacturers of stomach pills and laxatives will take over.

⚓

The Caravela d'Ouro is a café and a social club, on the second floor is a large restaurant. Downstairs at street level there is a counter, I order a cafè duplo descafeinado, carry the cup to a table in a corner. As soon as I sit down, I become invisible, able to observe everything around me. The room is noisy and full of life. Next door there is a playground. So the Caravela d'Ouro is a place where all the grandmothers, grandfathers, aunts, and nannies go with their children when the parents have to work to earn money. Four weathered men sit at a table, playing cards and sipping dark wine from small glasses. They play their game while the children frolic on the playground. One of these silverheads has a stack of 50-cent coins lying in front of him. If the grandchildren don't disturb him while he's playing, they are occasionally allowed to sit on the little locomotive next to the café, into which you toss a coin, and then it rocks a little and hisses a little. Small children are frozen with amazement, the older ones squeal with delight. Behind the scene, the yellow streetcars of the Eletrico No. 15 turn around to go back to the monastery, to the tourists and to Lisbon.

The journey can be the destination as I travel on "la linha" on the train from the Cais de Sodré to Cascais. In my head I form a story, which I will write down later. It is about a young man who gets on the train just before sunset to take pictures through the window. He notices that the windowpanes are dirty and scratched. But because he is a photographer, he takes pictures anyway. He believes it is his job to always photograph everything in front of his camera's eye, whether the conditions are good or not. While riding the train, he notices the many exotic trees standing majestically in the landscape. He tries to capture these magical creatures on film, as they say, but there is no film in his camera anymore, just a mass storage chip. Yes, the pictures aren't perfect, but after a while he notices that they are quite unusual and have their own beauty. Out of focus, at dusk, reflections of the neon lights show in the window. He suspects the result is going to be something special. He imagines himself exhibiting these photos, becoming famous with them, while every few seconds he aims at a tree from the fast-moving train, pushes the button, and waits for the next one. He imagines an art gallery in California, white walls, expensive people in exclusive clothes, and they admire his pictures. Then it's dark, the trees no longer stand out against the twilight, and the train pulls into the Cascais station. His fantasies disappear into the night, but it was exciting to dream of being an artist.

Christmas morning is the most beautiful time for me in Lisbon. The whole city is mine. There are no cars on the streets, all the stores, cafes, and restaurants are closed and families celebrate Christmas at home. I'm up early and I don't need stomach pills. Fortunately, the metro is running, less than ten passengers share the whole train. I get off at Olaias, just before the red line, a Linha Vermelha, leaves the underground tunnel to catch daylight for a few seconds. The station itself is a dream made real, in part looking like a steampunk comic book from a surreal future come to life, in part like a museum of poetry. At the top, on the street, I have a view of a colorful settlement of concrete castles, now lifeless like an abandoned set for a science fiction movie. A valley with steep slopes lies before me, a monastery, a railroad line, and huts where people dwell. Nobody is to be seen. My walk leads me along deserted six-lane streets and squares, past the Palace of the Pension Fund to the bullring Campo Pequeno, down the avenidas to Marques Pombal and the river. Meanwhile, the tourists are awake and I find a café where I get something to eat.

Very often, my daily routine as a writer begins early in the morning in the line to the café counter. The locals in front of me chat with the ladies behind the counter; some flirt. The small café stand in the shopping center Vasco da Gama buzzes with good humor, emanating especially from the young woman at the counter. A coffee-brown beauty with adventurously piled-up hair, flashing teeth, and a look that goes to heart and feet. She's always in the best of moods, and there's always something ironic about her, as if she doesn't even need the job. As if she only stands at this cash register at 7:30 in the morning because there's always something to laugh about. And because life in her villa with pool is just too boring.

After a few minutes of waiting and wondering, it's my turn. I don't speak the language well. Better said, I speak almost no word and understand almost nothing. So I describe in English how I would like my coffee. A double espresso in a coffee cup, extended with a little hot water. And sweetener, very important. I have developed a little choreography to go with my words. I show the double espresso with two fingers, represent the big cup with my right hand, and for the sweetener I hold up a small sachet that I carry in my wallet.

The ironic lady with the towering haircut looks at me with an amused benevolence. I'm never sure if she might be making fun of me. But it doesn't matter now. I am a pale, somewhat clumsy Northerner. Her gaze rests on me for a long second or two, then she calls out something to her colleagues that makes them laugh briefly. The woman at the mighty coffee machine goes about her work. The ironic lady holds out her hand. With a nod, she points to the display above the cash register, I may pay now, and pay respect.

Shortly thereafter, the coffee machine lady puts the

coffee on the counter, without the sweetener, though. I know where it is, so I bend low over the counter and fish two sachets of sweetener out of an old tin can. This is a bit brash and it is met with a frown that turns into a smile.

The café stand is located at the top of the mall on the gallery. From these tables I overlook everything, one of them is my personal table. Namely, the one that tilts the least. I get my laptop out of my backpack, drop the sweetener tablets into the crema and stir reverently. Just before I start writing, the two old men who come here every morning, also arrive. One scrawny and dried up like a twig, dressed in an old blue tracksuit, a baseball cap on his head. The other a fatty in a business suit. Both have a newspaper with them. They each look for a table, completely ignoring each other.

Another sip of coffee, creating a new document in Word - that's how my day as a writer begins. But I know that the most beautiful moment has already passed. That was when I was allowed to perform my coffee ordering routine in front of a strict and slightly amused audience. I read name of the coffee stand on the receipt, "Os Barões do Café", the Café Barons. That's why I call the cheerful women behind the counter my café baronesses.

⚓

I am writing the story of the photographer on the train, while I sit in the Jardim da Estrela. There's a laid-back water god here, plenty of rare plants, a pretty stone girl in a duck pond, exotic trees with roots like cables in a TV studio. There are a few tables around a kiosk that looks like a mushroom with its awnings, and to me it feels like paradise. If God really created a paradise, it was certainly inspired by the Estrela Park and the Gengibre da Estrela coffee mushroom. I watch a young man practicing on a slackline while I think about another young man photographing trees from a moving train. Many strollers stroll by, it could be an animated painting. The stone girl doesn't move. I write a line. I delete that line and write another. Time passes, and after a while I have really written something that I no longer delete.

⚓

It is just getting light over the Avenida da Liberdade, and in front of the luxury hotels, women and men in uniform are polishing the black limousines to perfection. Everything is expensive, the stores have been conquered by international luxury brands, and yet it is beautiful here, especially in the morning. The Avenida is a unique mixture of main street and small parks.

⚓

Casa Intendente is an enchanted, weathered, old mansion in the middle of that part of the city, where you hold your shoulder bag tighter hand and look around for dark figures in house entrances. In the large hall young people meet to speak and understand English. An American and a guy from Poland talk about train stations in Germany. A Portuguese woman tells the group how she expects to gain professional advantages in the bank where she works by speaking English. Many insider tips are exchanged. Lucy from Taiwan wears the reddest lipstick, matching her smile. She says, "You say, I'm beautiful. Well, that's a lazy and lousy way to describe me."

Above the Cacilhas lighthouse, the sky is so wide, so blue, that it should be enough for a lifetime. In the distance, Lisboa lies on the right side of the Tagus. The anglers at the lighthouse prefer to smoke and tell each other stories instead of paying attention to their fishing rods. So the fish have a chance, too. At the bus stop there is a group of pilgrims waiting for the bus to the Monument Christo Rei, where high above the hill a large statue of King Christ stands on a pillar, his head in the clouds. Here I arrived by ferry a few days ago, here I asked a young man to order me a cab in Portuguese with my phone, because all my waving never did any good. And this is where the story of a seductive mermaid takes place, who is actually a rivermaid. She asks a young man to buy her a burger in the restaurant with the two golden donkeys. In return, she wants to reward him with six kisses, and kisses from a river mermaid are something magical.

It's New Year's morning and my feet hurt from walking. The cafés are closed, I sit down in a church for a moment. White walls with large azulejo artworks on them. The church is empty, at this time the tourists are still sleeping. I close my eyes for a moment when I hear a strange noise. Someone is testing the loudspeakers. And then a Holy Mass begins with a singer and a song. I remain sitting quietly, not praying and not singing along. Instead, I listen intensely. The priest has a pleasant voice, the liturgy in Portuguese is beautiful. Suddenly my neighbor turns to me, an older woman in black. She shakes my hand, says something and smiles at me. She understands I don't know what to do, so she grabs me and hugs me tightly. After that, the other neighbors shake my hand too. I was not raised as a Catholic, so everything comes as a total surprise to me. I am very touched.

⚓

For a man who wants to play a writer, there is hardly a better place than Confeitaria Victória on Largo Dona Estefânia. Many small neon lights illuminate the room, the counter is full of pastries, men and women stand in front of it, quickly downing their coffee like medicine. Glass plates on the tables to protect the tablecloths. The air is full of voices, work colleagues, lovers, tourists telling each other what they have to tell each other. I sit in a corner and write a story about a writer who has just sent a novel to his editor and is now awaiting feedback. When shaving in his hotel he was still convinced he was a genius. In the meantime, all confidence has left him. Now he knows he hasn't written anything good. He will be laughed at. Surely his editor is looking for words to politely tell him that he is nothing but an impostor. The writer in my story is sitting at this very table in the *confeitaria* where I now sit and write. He watches the people at the counter as they quickly drink their coffee, and he wishes he were one of them, had a 9 to 5 job, a wife who loves him, who cooks him something to eat, and a couple of cute kids. How easy life would be then! He would have no reason for doubt. He would just be an ant and do what the other ants do. But he's an impostor, and soon everyone will know he can't really write. He thinks about buying a bottle of alcohol and getting drunk in the park. Then his phone notifies him that an email has arrived.

⚓

There is a large empty square between the shopping center and the East Station. At Christmas there are a few stalls where you can get barbecue, beer, wine, and schnapps. A kind of Christmas market, but very basic. While in the mall all the high-end brands are represented, here hardly any of the young vendors still have all their teeth. The country is torn into rich and poor, here I am reminded of that. Normally, the well-dressed hurry across the square to avoid being begged. But today a small band is playing by the stalls. Honestly, none of the musicians look like they have a home. But the music! Light Samba rhythms, wafting as if from a beach over the cold station forecourt at Christmas. The musicians come from all corners of the Lusophone world, from Angola, Brazil, Cape Verde, the Azores, and also the motherland of the Portuguese language. And then there are these beautiful women who are part of the band and move lasciviously like blades of grass in a light breeze. They are still young, yet scarred by hard life. Tonight they are stars, dancers who turn a cobbled square into a nightclub. That's where the well-dressed stop. There are a few extremely well-dressed, in garishly colored suits, with skin-tight silk dresses, and everyone sways along and lets themselves be enchanted. A family, proud father, young mother, the two small children also in suits. The father stands there watching the band with a smile, now and again someone comes and asks him for an autograph. Obviously he is not a stranger. More and more well-dressed people stop by and sink briefly into the music. In the stalls, lit by the neon, slices of pork are grilled, a little rosemary added and put in a bun, divine. Now the guitar whines for the last time, a woman collects money, the generator is switched off, the magic is over. What remains is an empty station forecourt, a whiff of pork and rosemary, and a reminder of the power of music.

Jürgen Schöneich

Note: The little dots above the vowels stand for "Umlaute". If for some reason they can't be written, an "e" is added to the Umlaut-vowels. On my credit card it says JUERGEN SCHOENEICH and that's perfectly ok with me.

Jürgen Schöneich (or) Juergen Schoeneich
born in Berlin, now lives in Hamburg, Germany. He writes for money whatever his clients wish — and short prose for free in his spare time. He became a member of the Lisbon Writing Group when staying in Lisboa as a tourist. Most of his writing is in his native tongue, the contribution to this anthology is his first publication in English. Find him on Facebook: https://www.facebook.com/juergen.schoeneich

Novena for St Anthony

Kate Tyte

St Antony was born in Lisbon in 1195. He is not the city's official patron saint, but he is the most popular. The 13th June is a city-wide holiday dedicated to him: an all-night street party, with a mass wedding, raunchy pimba music, grilled sardines, music and parades. St Anthony offers protection against shipwrecks and starvation, to fishermen and boatmen, travellers, the poor, the elderly, the sick and the oppressed. He is the patron saint of marriage and relationships, and the finder of lost things.

It is said that lost things will be returned to you if you tie a cord around the leg of your bed and repeat this prayer to the saint nine times.

*"The sea obeys and fetters break,
And lifeless limbs you do restore,
While treasures lost are found again,
When young or old your aid implore."*

One

The morning was washed fresh and clean by the terrors of the stormy night. We walked along the shoreline of Praia do Guincho, gathering tiny pale pink cowrie shells, each one glossy and shiny, into the palms of our hands. You find them after a storm, my father said, when the waves come rolling up from the depths, dragging the last treasures of the shipwrecks up from their watery graves. Somewhere out there in the Atlantic, the bones of slaves and sailors roll amongst caskets of gold, spices and beads, slowly releasing these tiny treasures one by one, into the hands of awaiting beachcombers.

Two

I first saw the poster stuck to the lamppost at the corner of Rua Cesario Verde, opposite Our Lady of Penha da Franca, a week ago. The missing cat was a big, brown tabby with white paws. I tore off the phone number on the strip, but secretly I thought there was no chance of finding that cat.

It's probably been run over, I thought, poor thing. I mean, when do you ever hear of missing cats being found? Then this morning, I was sitting in my back yard when I heard a commotion from upstairs. 'It's that cat!' my neighbour was shouting, pointing out of the window. I stood up and looked over the fence, and there it was, sunning itself on a shed roof. The owner was an old man, grey-haired and dignified, out of breath, but he took a chair from my kitchen and used it to clamber over the fence and onto the sheds. People leaned out of their windows to call out warnings and encouragement. The old man inched his way across the fragile tiles. The cat lazily stood, stretched, and moved further off. The old man continued his perilous journey, making kissy noises. 'Offer her some food!' I called. 'Look, a piece of cheese!' Eventually the cat consented to be scooped up and kissed by the old man, while the neighbourhood cheered. I took the cat from his arms so he could climb back over the fence, and I clutched her to my chest. She sat quite complacently, silky and hot from the sun. The next day the old man brought me a bouquet. They were lovely flowers.

Three

On the waste ground by the car park behind Rua Barao Sabrosa, amongst the purple bindweed, I find a headless statue of St Antonio. It's glazed blue, the small kind you see in every café, perched amongst the bottles of aguardente, the christ-child nestled in the arms of the monk. Women pray to the saint to send them a husband, but they forget to mention, a good husband. When the husband turns out bad, they cast the statues away. I move slowly over the rocky ground, searching for the tonsured head. If I find the head, I say to myself, if I find the head, and mend this statue, I will offer it up. I will go to church again. I will be good. Only bring him home. Bring him home and I will mend this thing that has been broken. I search and search amongst the weeds and the concrete rubble until it gets too dark to see.

Four

We found the phone in Jardim da Estrela, just sitting there on a bench, in a sparkly pink cover. There was nobody around. We debated what to do – should we go to the police, we wondered? – but finally we just took it with us. It was locked, of course. When it finally rang, the sound startled us, although we'd been expecting it. The girl was Russian and spoke haltingly in English. We agreed to meet back at the park, on one of the benches by the bandstand. She came running up to us waving, young and skinny, showered us with kisses, and ran off again, clutching the precious object.

Five

'Do you believe in god?' the man asks me, while the woman holding the leaflets nods encouragingly.

'Yes,' I say, 'yes I do, yes, of course I do.'

'Oh,' says the man.

Deprived of their prepared speeches they are too astonished to talk, and so am I. It's been decades since I've been to church. My father's funeral was the last time, I think. I had no idea where those words came from, they just bubbled up out of me. I walk on swiftly, leaving the leaflet holders on the pavement outside the pharmacy. A huge flock of pigeons takes off from the tree by the recycling bins in front of me. At six o'clock, they all gather at the corner of the street by Pastelaria Estrela de Paris, waiting for the baker to throw his tray of crumbs onto the pavement. I turn my startling words over in my mind. Do I believe in god? Yes I do, I think to myself, yes I do. I feel lighter than I have in years. The city is beautiful, the pigeons are beautiful, even the stench of the overflowing bins reminds me I am alive. When I pass the church, I look up and give a little nod of acknowledgement. But I don't go in.

Six

I was standing in the queue for more sangria, jostled by the crowds, who squeezed past on both sides in their wigs shaped like tonsured monk's heads or pots of basil. The air was full of bluish smoke and the smell of charcoal burners and sardines. Looking down the steps it was just a heaving mass of people: dancing, walking, drinking, eating. A rotund man in an embroidered waistcoat and a little porkpie hat was standing on a small stage with his keyboard. He started up a new pimba song, and the whole crowd around me joined in with the chorus, yelling out,'*Abraco, braco com ela!*' and I noticed the man in front of me wiping a tear off his cheek. His companion put his arms around him, and they stood there, swaying together, while the crowd sang on.

Seven

The student is a woman in her fifties, smartly dressed, with perfectly styled hair. It's the worst age to begin studying again. She's often late, flustered, apologising, rushing out to answer phone calls from work. She has two teenage sons, a sick mother, and sometimes fans herself vigorously with her textbook while the younger students look confused. During the first class she's nervous, so nervous she rushes out of the room and cries a little in the corridor. But week after week, she comes to class. School was obviously a traumatic experience for her. Things were different back then. She hints as much. She doesn't want to take the final test, tells me she feels sick at the thought. Nevertheless she takes the test. She fails. I consider it a huge victory. I tell her so. See you again next term, I tell her. She nods. You're one of my success stories, I say. She smiles. I think she knows that I mean it.

Eight

Recent things are the first to go: appointments, grocery shopping, her glasses, whether or not she's had lunch. Then she forgets what we did last week and starts to get upset that we never visit her. I was here yesterday, I say gently, but she doesn't believe me. She phones me at strange times of day, telling me that somebody has stolen her can opener. You don't need a can opener, I say, the cans have ring pulls on them now. Then she loses the names of her grandchildren. She's retreating backwards into the familiar world of her youth, as though her adult years never existed. I sit by the bed and hold her hand, the skin as fragile as tissue paper over the thick purple veins. 'Dolly was here,' she says. 'She was so good. She didn't bark at all, she just stayed here with me.' Dolly was her parents' dog when she was little; she must have been gone for sixty or seventy years now. These things are lost: her husband, her children, the names of familiar objects, whole decades of her life. These things remain: Dolly's stiff, bristly fur; the smooth metal pan her mother used to cook in, dented and worn thin; the feel of the cow's tongues, rough on her hands as she fed them handfuls of dry grass; a small wooden doll with a painted face; the pattern the sunlight made as it filtered through the vines shading the terrace.

Nine

When I first moved to the city, it was in the grip of a heatwave that lasted well into November. I moved through the sweating air as slowly as the black-clad old ladies navigating the stairways cut into the steep hillsides. In the afternoons, I went out to the ice-cream shop in the square at Campo Ourique, working my way through the flavours: pistachio, apricot, watermelon, pineapple, raspberry. I chose the combinations based on their beautiful colours. The cicadas shrieked in the trees and the ice cream melted faster than I could eat it. The shop closed during the quarantine. It never re-opened.

Kate Tyte

Kate Tyte was born in Bath, England. She worked as an archivist for over ten years, before moving to Lisbon where she works as an English teacher. Her non-fiction has appeared in various British history and genealogy magazines. Her essays have appeared in *Slightly Foxed*, and her fiction and poetry in *STORGY*, *Riggwelter*, *Idle Ink*, *The Fiction Pool*, *Press Pause Press* and the anthologies *Ghastly Gastronomy*, and *Strange Spring: Stories We Wrote in Self-Isolation*, and on the podcast *The Other Stories*. She is a book reviewer for *STORGY* and *The Short Story*.

Alive in Lisbon

Marianne Rogoff

My hotel is as I pictured it, simple with all the comforts: nice bed, private bath (with bidet and tub), phone, desk, and best: a sweet terrace with a wide-angle view of the red-tile roofs of the vast city of Lisbon. The light of late afternoon is soft-focus and otherworldly. At night, circus/calliope rhythms reach my windows from a courtyard below, where a large group of teenagers practice a line dance: march, grapevine, side-step, swing your partner, singing along in Portuguese.

Leaving in the morning on foot from the inn's hilltop perch near Miradouro do Monte means following a winding path downhill through Graça and Alfama's narrow neighborhood streets. Looking into doorways, walking the cobbled alleys, I lose track of how to retrace my steps, and can only go forward, on a self-paced stroll with no destination. Glimpses of Tagus River provide orientation and I head toward the water to get my bearings. My new beaded sandals work well on the stones: stable ground. Knee-length skirt a comfort, glad to have sweater on turns into sudden gusts. I walk along the wide riverfront boulevard toward Municipal Plaza, and now I appreciate being where tourists are expected. The pedestrian shopping street, Rua Agosto, leads to Rossio Plaza and a stop for *café con natas* at a sidewalk café for people watching.

I sit among street musicians, beggars, tourists, and artists. Here I am, author of *Silvie's Life*, story of the life and death of my baby girl, now a book adopted for courses on end-of-life ethics and the right to die, translated into Portuguese. My publisher has invited me to speak at four venues in Portugal, and agreed to pay my flight and three nights hotel but I have no *cheque* in hand yet, and so I worry a little about everything.

I observe the Human Statue at work nearby his collection jar, standing on a high box, white garb draped at length so he appears extra tall, in white face, white hands, cloth wrapped like gauze, facial expression of a sad clown. A crowd gathers, awaiting his act. But the act is simply this: to stand perfectly still, be like Pessoa, no one, empty, a blank canvas on whom the observer can toss a personality, empty so perhaps a soul can appear.

At the corner: a mysterious figure seated on a doorstep: Is he wearing a mask? What does it signify? What does he mean for us to make of it, to think?

A closer look reveals that it is the man's face, his actual face! Visible purple and red tumors, bursting vessels twice as big as his face, grow there obscuring his humanity. Attempting to understand what I'm seeing, I catch his eye, barely detectible amidst the raw red clay of his face.

He has eyes! He's human!

Not soulless like the white-draped statue, but fully present, and stricken by this disease, his fate, which renders him a beggar. Who could love such a being? I do, I love him; the eye connects his humanity to mine. I drop all my coins and bills in his upturned palm then join a stream of others passing by him without stopping.

Later, I describe him to my doctor hosts and learn it is true, there is nothing that medicine can do for his particular affliction. The society of neonatologists wants to know why this is so: why do some newborns arrive with *anomalias* – defects, predispositions, imbalances – that will render their lives miserable or short, or both? Death is everyone's fate, but the whims and will of expected natural order include this percentage of chaos and extremes at the edges of commonness.

Doctors do not respond with the "why" of philosophy, literature, or religion; they face off anomalies with science, analyze statistics for where and why there arise clusters of experience, use microscopes to examine close-up the details of the misshaped kidney, trace back in sonograms to which prenatal period initiates the "wrong turn," present findings in PowerPoints in darkened hotel conference rooms (as outside the sun blazes, wind pushes air, waves pound the rocky Viana do Castelo coast). The audience takes notes. Where can the doctor intervene to prevent this, or if not, to treat it, to right the wrong? Research is assessed, conclusions offered: these are the possibilities; this is what we might be able to control. The rest – what is out of control – is not the subject of these meetings.

I am introduced into the conversation to tell my story. My memoir *Silvie's Life* has been translated as *Estar Grávida É Estar de Esperanças.* "Being pregnant is called expecting," the first sentence of *Silvie's Life,* has become the Portuguese title. I read from a chapter set in the Neonatal Intensive Care Unit (NICU), a place I call "God out of control," and my book says, "This is not supposed to happen."

My daughter's case was extreme. After ten days of tests, trauma, and assessment, doctors concluded she had suffered severe brain damage and that death was "her best hope." Our task as parents became how to accomplish this within the boundaries of law, morality, and our infinite love for our newborn.

"We needed an explanation. No one could explain it," I read.

Does the distinguished lady doctor wearing the cross necklace cringe when I call God out of control? *Silvie's Life* wonders what kind of faith can allow for belief in a God who designs *anomalias,* or, if not designs them, permits them to exist?

Belief that suggests this is part of our lesson here? *Imperfection.*

Only God is perfect? – and maybe even God is still learning.

⚓

The churches of Portugal are fortresses, walls three feet thick, interiors a kind of hubris, prideful reaching toward some perceived conferred power – priests' throne-like seats, bishops' tombs, velvet robes, worship-me rituals. I feel both awe and cynicism inside these monuments to power.

The University of Coimbra's grand plaza overlooks the city and river, and to step inside the ancient library requires an appointment. My group enters the temperature-controlled, sacred space with its ladders to high shelves, books in cages, grand conformity of spines and colors, grand depository of knowledge on medicine, law, physics, mathematics, the arts. Climbing through the buildings, the steps are unevenly sunken and slippery from thousands of footprints, weight of centuries; I can feel my fleeting presence and my permanent mark as well.

⚓

At Café Brasileira in Lisbon, Portugal's most famous poet, Fernando Pessoa, appears as a bronze man in a hat and suit seated at a bronze outdoor café table, with an empty seat where everyone who passes feels compelled to sit and pose for photos. I regard this parade: the traveler observes, the writer records these observations, the ordinary person wants her picture taken with Pessoa, and I hand my camera to a café neighbor, gesturing the shutter click as we don't speak the same language.

Then I enter the café and head toward the back to watch comings and goings. All is chatter, animated, relaxed, nothing going on that doesn't happen here on any given afternoon. I see four men enter through the front doorway; one pushes the other, who returns a punch to the shoulder, which causes the first one to stumble then retaliate. Portuguese is tossed in the air, some insult or threat, then the four go at it, a regular *brouhaha,* and the patrons shout, stand up from their seats (myself among them), as the tinkle of breaking glass is heard – the mirror at the entrance? glass in the doors? port glasses at tables? A roar goes up, the waiters shout, one hurls a bottle at them, the bartender is on the phone to *Policia* as is the fat lady on her cell.

Outside, there is a row of sidewalk cafés full of people who leap up shouting as the men "take it outside," and proceed with the fight down the block.

Inside, the café settles into an excited bustle – Ah, how the energy of the afternoon can change, the moment of danger reinvigorates the ordinary; emotional tenor shifts.

We've just dodged "what could have happened" (one pulls a gun, or the tumble falls in my direction; I am, after all, trapped in the back of the café, the fight at its entrance; we were all forced to witness and wait to see where danger might strike, be prepared to defend our space and lives). Everyone is shaking their heads, reliving excitement, speculating, dismissing the men as ruffians, laughing about it now; fear gone and replaced with some new elation that coffee and wine can't offer. Only the adrenalin of fear gives this spark.

One afternoon in my small hotel lobby I overhear the clerk, José Manuel, describing his "problem child" to someone on the phone. Later, we talk to each other and I show him my book, "This is why I'm here." (He speaks some English; I employ my little Portuguese.) Soon, he is pulling pictures from his wallet, one of his son now at age five, and the dreaded NICU shot with his newborn attached to all the tubes and wearing the too-familiar cap and blanket with the same pink and turquoise stripes used in the U.S.

I gulp. "Yes, my baby looked like this. But listen, her situation was extreme. She didn't live."

His baby, his boy, lives, and his challenges will be ongoing. (I don't diagnose but it sounds like autism, or obsessive-compulsive disorder; José Manuel calls him *hyperactive)*. He and his wife disagree about how to respond, and I worry for their marriage; I've been through all this, death and divorce, and feel like I'm on the other side. I have Dale, my wonderful healthy son, and many blessings: good work, great health, many communities.

I point to Teresa Botelho's name in the Preface to *Estar Grávida É Estar de Esperanças*, "Maybe she can help you; she works with these children and families."

José Manuel has no faith in psychologists, he says, he doesn't read books, but accepts my gift of the book, maybe for his wife.

On Monday morning I am scheduled to tour the public hospital with Teresa Botelho, Maria do Ceu Machado, who wrote the other preface, and Alexandra Dias, my translator. Dr. Machado heads the Department of Pediatrics and Neonatology; Dr. Botelho leads the psychology team; Dr. Dias is a respected pediatrician.

Two young psychologists-in-training accompany us as we visit the children's library and play room, staff offices, wards, and intensive care. We pass through waiting rooms for day service appointments, noisy with hordes of the needy, all races.

It is a squelching hot day and the hospital is not an air-conditioned place; the air is stifling with the smell of bodies, illness, and fear. On the wards, there is the smell of bleach and disinfectants; in the cafeteria, hospital food. My hosts, used to the smells, the air, the sight of the needy hordes, walk past as if guiding me through a cathedral or museum, casually (kindly, respectfully) pointing out children with pneumonia, those with long-term care needs, one with possible lymphoma or is it edema that will respond to medication given one more day?

All is well, *tudo bem,* I'm in stride, okay, until I'm invited in, inside, in closer, to see the newborns in their cubicles. Alone in a blanketed cubby, there's Matilda, teeny, bruised, connected by wires, holding on by a thread, alive. Breathing!

I bend close to peer inside, a spectator, and feel ashamed for looking, for being on tour. Gulps of emotion are swallowed then rise like air as I cross the room to meet the young Portuguese mother hovering lovingly over her perfectly beautiful baby boy. He is so so small, desperately yet calmly attempting to live with his intricate hands and complex brain waves, internal organs striving to do their work of coming into life and sustaining life before he is fully formed and ready. He has been here three months so far. This mother has been here, too, in this darkened room with the busy nurses, doctors, and monitors, in love with this new being, faithfully conjuring hopeful thoughts.

This is when I start to cry, seeing that young mother. Looking into the more dire condition of the fist-sized African preemie, grasping a hand in camaraderie with the stoic, broad mother, I mumble, *"Compreendo,* I understand." I want to offer hopeful prayers, can only extend my love.

As we exit, a deep well of old feelings engulfs me as I fall, weeping, down the well.

My guides seem surprised and I am, too.

"I'm so sorry, it's been 18 years, I did not expect to feel this way."

"You haven't been in a NICU since?"

"No."

Why would I?

I ran as far from the place as I could get, avoided all thoughts of this becoming my life's work. Yet I wrote *Silvie's Life,* and attention was being paid to her story, again, after all these years, and it is my work here now.

One neonatologist down the hall realizes it's me, the famous author, here in their midst, and hurries over, drops everything to catch up with me, to tell me, *this is an important book* – she read it last week on a plane, because she heard I would be here – how meaningful it is for doctors to hear from the patient's side of the bed.

Someone has brought me tissues and I stand in the hallway dabbing at eye makeup, as I try to absorb this praise. Aware that I could sob all day, bottomless buckets even after all this time, I recuperate enough to move through the cafeteria line with these fine people, swallow a few mouthfuls of bad food, attempt to keep track of conversation about the newest baby in crisis.

My other appointment on my last day in Lisbon is at the offices of Gradiva Publishers with the formal Sr. Begonha, who has most efficiently arranged for my *cheque.* Generous Sr. Begonha inquires how I'll spend the rest of the day.

"Wander the neighborhood, drink coffee; try to process everything that's happened."

Sr. Begonha locates a city map and highlights his recommended path to tranquility, then walks me to the corner and his favorite café, points downhill to *Jardin do Estrela* (with its beautiful, shaded benches to rest on, gazebo, and wide walking paths), and beyond to his secret garden – *Jardin Botanica,* an oasis of palm trees, labyrinth hedges, and giant-root ancient *arbols.* There, in the silence at the center of Lisbon city, I will find a shaded bench and release all my tears, shed mascara, snot, and façades of composure.

I will cry for many reasons, not least my pleasure and shock that my deceased baby girl herself has led me here, to this dark green garden. *Silvie,* her fictional name, connects to the word *sylvan,* meaning, green dark forest. *A-ha.* Her mother will smile at the image of herself, wetly weeping in a garden in the city of Lisbon, so far from home; she'll blow her nose, wipe sweat, and persist in walking through the heat onward toward the rest of her life.

⚓

Back at the hotel I pay my bill with the Gradiva *cheque,* shy around José Manuel. Business settled, he says, "I read your book today."

"The whole book?"

"Yes. In three sessions. I had to stop when guests arrived, of course, and when I cried."

His experience was exactly the same in the beginning, he tells me; it brought all the memories back. "But of course my son is alive, and for that I can be grateful."

Guests come in and need his attention. José Manuel nods to me, embraces my hand, and I bow good night. *Boa noite*.

I ride the elevator to the rooftop bar and buy two bottles of water to drink in my room while I ponder the extravagant nighttime view. Outside, the calliope dance loudly proceeds.

Marianne Rogoff

"Alive in Lisbon" was previously published in Marianne Rogoff's Pushcart-nominated story collection *Love Is Blind in One Eye* and won a Bronze Solas Award from Travelers Tales, who included the story in *The Best Women's Travel Writing 2008*. She first visited Lisbon and fell in love when her memoir *Silvie's Life* was translated into Portuguese by Gradiva Publishers in 2006. During winter and summer breaks from teaching, she leads weeklong trips for writers to exotic locales. Portugal is, of course, high on the list. Visit mariannerogoff.com to be invited!

White Rabbit of Lisbon

Marina Pacheco

Branca Coelho snapped her pocket watch shut as the metro pulled into Cais do Sodré station. It was one minute and thirty-two seconds late. It probably didn't matter, but it made her tense. She stepped out onto the platform, clutching her small brown suitcase, paused for a fraction to take in the three-story-high murals of her ancestor, the White Rabbit of Alice in Wonderland, rushing towards the exit and loped off in the same direction.

She'd come by metro because she found it reassuring. Her particular fondness for tubes, tunnels, and metro systems ran through every link of her DNA. No trip to a foreign city was complete without a visit to their underground. She'd seen almost all the greats. New York was stifling hot, stark, plastic, and stripped to the bare essentials. London, the oldest of the lot, clung to its Victorian heritage with mostly narrow winding tunnels and tight platforms. St Petersburg was a palace to commuting with ballroom-sized platforms, murals, mosaics, and chandeliers. Lisbon was newer, smaller, but well thought out and comfortable. The only one on her must-see list that hadn't been checked off yet was Tokyo. She shuddered at the idea of a train packed so tightly they employed people to shove commuters inside. Still, it had to be a sight to behold.

Branca bounded up the stairs, the escalator was always too slow for her, and out into the depressing raw concrete station. It was such a comedown from the attractive Metro below. At least it meant she wasted no time getting outside. She stepped sideways, out of the way of the commuters, mostly humans but with a few other species, and took a deep fortifying breath as she looked about. She couldn't spot any relatives, friends, or nosy neighbours who might run home to tell tales.

The light from the hot summer sun bounced off the small, brilliant-white square cobbles and dazzled Branca. No city in the world had more beautiful pavements, mostly white but often with trailing, curvaceous, inlaid black patterns. She loved every inconvenient, slippery-as-hell bit of them.

She joined a crowd of tourists and locals waiting for the traffic light to get her across the four lanes of the Avenida 24 Julho. As it turned green, she dashed across, making for the shade of the small trees that dotted the plaza opposite. It was so hot she was wearing a billowy cotton sundress with a tiny pink and blue rose pattern. She also had her largest floppy hat, partially for camouflage. Although there would be no hiding her ears that poked through a pair of holes and did a good job of keeping the hat on her head.

She decided to cut through the warehouse-like Timeout food market. Usually she would give it a miss because it was full of tourists. But it was still early, and emptier nowadays, what with all the hygiene restrictions. Today it was also cooler, and she skirted the stalls, barely noticing the mouthwatering food laid out like gems in a jewelry store. She had no time for that. She had to keep on her toes and not be spotted.

Then she was out into the blazing sun again. She crossed the green square that was the Jardim don Luis, past the red bandstand-like kiosk providing the locals with their mid-morning coffees, up another block, and she was at the arched stone entrance to the tram elevator.

What had once been a public service to help locals get up a street so steep the pavement was stepped, had turned into a tourist attraction. Nowadays it was so rammed with sightseers that the locals had gone back to walking up. A narrow, shady staircase led up along the side of the tram's garage and opened onto a landing, another flight of stairs, another landing, and then the one-person-wide pavement with the stairs all the way to the top of the Calçada da Bica Pequena.

Branca didn't mind stairs. In fact, she enjoyed hopping up them and bounded her way past the tiny windows and doors of the yellow and blue painted homes that opened directly out onto the street. She paused as a tourist-laden, tiny, bright-yellow tram screeched by before continuing her climb past the shops and Hairport, the most avant garde of Lisbon's hairdressers.

She'd once had her snowy white fur dyed pink there, much to the horror of her numerous relatives. Most of them were on the conservative side and Branca tried not to send them into a tailspin of disapproval too often.

Heaven alone knew what they'd think of today's assignation. Actually, no, she knew exactly what reaction she would get. That was why she'd chosen to meet in the east of Lisbon, where she was least likely to run into any of her extended family.

She turned left, took the broad staircase three steps at a time, and turned left again at the top onto a street lined by what were once elegant, stately, family homes. Now they were hotels, offices, and, right at the end, a museum. The Pharmacy Museum, to be precise.

She was high up here and the plaza opened out to offer a superb view of the mighty Tejo River and the red 25 de Abril suspension bridge that crossed it. The intense green leaves of the row of mature trees shone against the pale blue sky. It was as if the summer heat drained the sky of colour because it was always a more saturated blue in the spring.

Branca's whiskers twitched with edgy excitement as she walked through the welcoming, wide-open, wrought-iron gates. She scanned the tables that were spread out across a broad terrace and lower garden that belonged to the museum's restaurant. It was slightly pricier than most of the other local eateries, but worth it for the atmosphere and the view. They also had a chef who liked to experiment with interesting variations on traditional Portuguese cuisine.

Branca plumped for a table on the terrace. It felt a little exposed, but she was determined not to be cowed by the situation. She would be careful, certainly, but not paranoid. Not today, the most important day of her life.

Branca perused the menu while she waited, flapping her hat in front of her face because it was still hot in the shade of the big red umbrella. She looked up and her heart skipped a beat in combined fear and anticipation each time somebody walked through the gate. But so far, it had only been couples, or trios and quartets of friends. She checked her phone for a message. There were none. She resisted looking at her pocket watch. It only made it feel like time slowed down.

She was about to check for messages again when Vicente strolled through the gate. Branca gave a happy gasp, thrilled and relieved to see him. She couldn't help thinking, as she did whenever she saw him, that he was the most handsome raven alive.

Unlike everybody else, who were dressed casually and with the minimum to remain decent and cope with the heat, Vicente was wearing a grey linen suit and a crisp white shirt that contrasted magnificently against his jet-black feathers. The only thing that made him look slightly casual was the black leather rucksack currently slung over his right shoulder.

'I hope I haven't kept you waiting?' Vicente murmured as he got close and tilted his head to examine her with one inky black eye.

'Not at all,' Branca said, leaped to her feet, and then stopped. Flinging her arms around him out in the open like this was probably not a good idea. 'I've been enjoying the view.'

Vicente glanced back and gave it a slight nod. He could fly. For him, this view was probably rather pedestrian. That didn't matter, because he'd sat down and was examining her gravely.

'Are you alright?' he asked.

'A little nervous.'

Branca had more reason to be nervous than Vicente did. She came from a vast family. Not many people know this, but rabbits come from the Iberian Peninsula. There were thousands, if not hundreds of thousands, of them in Lisbon and most were related, if not by birth, then by marriage. It was different for Vicente. He was an only child from parents who had been the last of the ravens of Lisbon.

His lineage couldn't be better, though. It was his ancestors who had sailed into Lisbon harbour centuries ago on a little boat bearing the body of Saint Vicente. He'd become the patron saint of Lisbon, and the two accompanying ravens were memorialised in the city's black and white crest.

Her family wouldn't give a snap of the fingers about that, though. They'd say, correctly, that Coelho was one of the oldest surnames in Portugal. Not only that, but he wasn't a rabbit, and that was all there was to it. If they discovered what she was up to now, they'd do everything in their power to stop her.

Vicente reached across the table to take her paw and said, 'It will be fine.'

'As long as you're here,' Branca said, warmed all the way to the tips of her ears by his smile.

'Have you ordered yet?'

'I was waiting for you.'

'I think, today, we should have champagne.'

'Afterwards,' Branca said. 'Once it's done and we're safe.'

Vicente examined her gravely and said, 'Are you still sure you want to do this?'

'Oh I am, with all my heart.'

'We ravens mate for life, you know. If I was to lose you....' he trailed off, unable to finish.

'I will never love another male as long as I live. I have no doubts about what we are going to do. I'm just worried about my family.'

He knew. They'd discussed it often enough. She'd even tried sounding out her parents just after her eldest sister had given birth to twins, a boy and a girl. Her sister's husband was an exceedingly handsome, piebald rabbit who had the additional felicity of being a wealthy lawyer. With so much joy in the house, she'd decided to tentatively float the idea of interspecies marriage.

The silence her vague query brought to the house was bad enough. Her mother's shocked expression and whispered, 'Branca... no!' had been altogether worse.

So she'd laughed it off and pretended it was a mischievous, hypothetical question. The family had accepted her explanation a little too eagerly, but there was discomfort when they went back to fawning over the first grandchildren born to her family. Branca had never returned to the subject.

'So what would you like for your pre-wedding brunch?' Vicente asked, trying to act lighthearted.

It didn't suit him. His was a grave and sombre personality. Branca always said he grounded her. She tended to be flighty.

'Full of fun,' Vicente said.

She was the yin to his yang, a pair in perfect harmony, each balancing the other out.

'Let's have something grand. I like the look of the carrot cake.'

'Carrot cake for you,' Vicente said. 'I'll have the open salmon sandwich. And if not champagne, then let's at least have a sparkling wine.'

'Why not?' Branca said, beaming up at Vicente. He always made her feel safer and more relaxed. Now that he was here, she had no doubt the rest of the day would go smoothly.

It was probably nerves, and definitely too much sparkling wine, that left Branca lightheaded as she and Vicente made their way down a shady road towards the church. She was so wobbly she wanted to hang onto Vicente. She could draw some courage from him at the same time. But he'd insisted on taking her suitcase as well as his luggage, so he was now rather weighed down.

Her suitcase held a frothy white veil, the only concession towards wedding clothes, and something for their honeymoon. They'd be taking a train ride north to a lovely old Quinta in Peneda Gerês. It was modest, but neither of them wanted to attract attention and travel nowadays was fraught with difficulty, so they opted for something simple and easy.

A thrill of excitement shivered its way up from her belly button. She was happy. Despite what might happen later with her relatives, for now she was hopping along beside the male she loved and they were going to get married. That was good enough for her.

They turned left into a typical Lisbon street comprised of solid blocks of buildings separated only by roads. The 300-year-old façades of the three- to five-story buildings were either tiled with blue dominating the patterns, or painted in traditional white, pink, or yellow. The balconies, many of them rusted to the point where Branca wouldn't risk walking out onto them, were curving wrought-iron creations, partly obscured by a crisscross of telephone and power lines overhead. The pavement wasn't wide enough for the two of them to walk side by side and whenever they met someone coming the other way they had to step out into the road to pass each other, risking being flattened by a stream of cars and the occasional trundling tram.

'We're nearly there,' Vicente said, glancing back at her and now even he looked nervous, but tempered with excitement.

He was as happy as her that this moment had nearly arrived. It was thanks to his saintly family background and church connections that they were about to be married in the fabulous Igreja Santa Catarina. He'd been able to skip the waiting list that had expanded to beyond a year due to local popularity and Covid restrictions.

The Igreja Santa Catarina was a lesser-known gem of a church that was seldom visited by tourists. Its austere façade with the white twin bell towers provided the only hint that it was a church and not just some grand building in a row of grand buildings.

'They're there, look,' Branca said, nearly jumping up and down in her excitement.

They, were Pedro Javalie and his wife Graça. Pedro was an impressive wild boar, the epitome of his species, with intimidatingly broad shoulders, curling dark ivory tusks, and a ridge-like mane of black hair that he'd tried to paste down with hair gel and only been partially successful with. Graça was a beautiful, dappled white and brown goat, who was dressed in an old-fashioned but smart linen suit.

Pedro and Graça had been married for five years already. They were active in the cross- species community. They provided support, a shoulder to cry on, sensible advice, and sometimes accommodation for any couples who ended up being kicked out of their family for their transgressions. They'd helped Branca and Vicente understand what their families might do and the best way to deal with any fallout.

'Every family is different, and every mixed couple will go about how they break the news and what they do next in their own way. There is no right and wrong, just an attempt to keep what ties you can or want, and otherwise live your own lives in a happy and fulfilled way.'

Branca found them both reassuring, especially the way they managed to get over their problems.

'We bond over food,' Pedro said with a laugh once when Branca had asked him how they did it. 'Neither of us are fussy eaters.'

'An understatement,' Vicente had murmured with a knowing smile cast at Branca.

Now, Pedro and Graça were here to be their support and, most importantly, witnesses for the marriage.

'At least our families will be pleased we got married in church,' Branca said as she reached their friends.

'Here,' Graça said, handing Branca a posy of white flowers, slightly nibbled on one side, 'for the bride.'

'Thank you,' Branca said, breathless now that the

moment had arrived.

'You'll be fine,' Graça said and put a gentle hoof against Branca's back to guide her up the stairs, through the meters-deep archway to the narrow veranda and then through into the church itself.

It was cool, smelt strongly of frankincense, and was so dim it took Branca's eyes a while to adjust. She'd been here before to meet the priest so she knew what to expect; all the same, the ornate rococo-style church still had the power to awe from its golden, many-piped organ that dominated the floor above as if floating halfway up the wall to the pastel pink and blue, arched ceiling ornamented with gilt and white plaster filigree, and the regularly spaced side chapels that ran the length of the church and whose many columned walls, statues, and altars were entirely coated in gold.

A little group huddled around the altar. More friends from the cross-species community. A human man and his sinuous grey-striped cat wife, a mouse and a rat, who surprisingly had the greatest difficulties reconciling their families with their union, and a horse and a donkey.

Vicente and Branca had long ago discussed and come to terms with the fact that they would never be able to have children of their own. Even adoption would be difficult for beings with such different cultural backgrounds. But Branca thought that was better than the horse and the donkey, who could have children but knew their offspring would be infertile. It hardly seemed fair to the kids. That was such a fraught subject it was rarely touched upon in their group counselling sessions or at less-formal get-togethers.

'Are you ready?' Father Almeida asked from his position in front of the altar.

The priest was dressed in the traditional white wedding vestments embroidered in gold that far outshone what Branca was wearing. He was now blinking anxiously at Vicente and Branca through the thick circular lenses of his glasses that made his pale moon-like face look even rounder. Part of the reason he's agreed to officiate this wedding was because Vicente had promised they'd be quick.

So Branca whipped off her hat and took her veil out of her little suitcase where she'd laid it right on top. Then she hopped down the aisle, pulling the veil into place and fluffing it out. Vicente hopped along beside her so that the two of them arrived, slightly breathless before the priest as their friends closed about them. Pedro stood beside Vicente and Graça was on Branca's left beaming at her.

'Are we all here?' Father Almeida said.

He'd had the situation explained to him. While he'd expressed his concerns over the clandestine nature of the wedding and the absence of either the brides or groom's family, he'd nevertheless agreed to go ahead with the ceremony. Branca was grateful to him for that and for the fact that he didn't bring it up again today.

'You look beautiful,' Vicente murmured.

It gave Branca a thrill and helped to settle her nerves. She'd been told all brides suffered from butterflies and last-minute anxieties. That was fine. Most of her fears were focused outwards. What she wouldn't give to be a normal bride and have her father accompany her up the aisle.

The priest started the wedding service and Branca pushed that thought away. She'd spent hours thinking about the pros and cons of her marriage over the last few months, through the support group and even during the church marriage lessons. Not once, in all that time, had she thought what she was doing was a mistake.

'If anyone knows of a reason these two can't be married, speak now or forever hold your peace,' Father Almeida said and spent, in Branca's opinion, far too long waiting for a reply.

Her heart thumped away in her chest like a rabbit pounding a full-scale alarm to the entire group. This was the part of the wedding she'd been most worried about. What little sleep she'd got last night had been filled with nightmares of her family leaping out of hiding at this very moment to put an end to her marriage.

But there was just silence. Father Almeida nodded and his complacent expression was of a man who'd said the same thing thousands of times and never had an objection.

He moved on to the exchange of vows and rings. And finally he said, 'I now pronounce you husband and wife,' and broke into a benevolent smile.

'No!' an angry shout came from the main doors.

Branca swung round as rabbits swarmed into the church and bounded down the main aisle and even over the pews towards her and Vicente. Her father led the charge, his face set in a furious scowl.

'It's alright,' Vicente said, stepping in front of Branca. 'I will protect you.'

The rest of the wedding party did the same, forming a defensive line.

'There are so many. You'll never be able to hold them all off,' Branca gasped.

Even as she spoke her father arrived at the barricade of friends and set to hopping up and down in one place trying to find her.

'Branca, don't do this,' he yelled as he spotted her. 'No-one in our family has ever married outside our species.'

'There's a first time for everything,' Branca shouted back. She had to calm down enough to remember all the words she'd rehearsed for when she did tell her family. 'Vicente and I love each other.'

'How can you do this?' her mother shouted.

She was alternating her bounce with Branca's father so that she first saw her mum, and then her dad, and then her mum again over Pedro Javali's broad shoulders. Seconds later, Branca also spotted her sister and brother-in-law pummelling at the horse and the donkey with their powerful hind legs. That, she knew, was incredibly painful. Stop it,' Branca cried. 'It's the modern world and we live in a city. Species of all kinds are getting along better than ever before. Please, just give me a chance to explain.'

'After you went sneaking off without telling us what you were up to?Mum shouted, and with an almighty effort she vaulted over Pedro, using his shoulder for leverage and landed in the gap between Branca and Vicente. 'I can't allow this.'

'I'm sorry,' Vicente said, pulling Branca behind himself. 'But you are too late to prevent it.'

Branca was touched that he would defend her. He was apparently ready to fight because he'd stripped out of his jacket and was in the process of unbuttoning his snowy white shirt.

'Nothing's been signed yet. It isn't official till you sign the register,' Mum said, with a triumphant spark in her eye.

'It won't make any difference,' Branca said. 'I won't leave Vicente, even if we aren't officially married. We just wanted to make a statement to the world of our love. That's why we decided on a church wedding.'

'It's an abomination,' Mum cried and tried to leap over Vicente.

But he wrapped one feathered wing around Branca and spun her away from her mother.

'What do you want to do now?' Vicente murmured in her ear.

'They're in no mood to talk. I'll never be able to calm them down.'

'Then we should leave,' Vicente said as he pulled his other wing out of his shirt and flapped, sending powerful eddies of wind through the church.

To Branca it felt as though a black-winged angel had suddenly appeared.

'Yes, let's go. Otherwise people will get hurt,' Branca said and leaped onto Vicente's back.

'Hold tight,' he said gravely.

Branca had only been for a flight once with Vicente and that had been in the Sintra mountains where they had plenty of room. She leaned forward into Vicente's soft, warm feathers and wrapped her arms around his neck.

He leaped into the air on a powerful downbeat of his wings that shot them straight up. Seconds before, the ceiling had seemed so high that the painted fresco images were tiny. Now Branca was practically face to face with a life-sized cherub.

'No!' the crowd below shouted.

The hordes of rabbits that filled the nave looked like fluffy toys from up here. It also seemed like all her uncles, aunts, and cousins had turned out for the intervention.

'There's too many of them,' Branca said. 'How will we get out?'

'Leave that to me,' Vicente said as he swooped around the painted ceiling.

He aimed for the double doors of the church, snapped his wings shut, and the two of them shot like a rocket through the door. Vicente's momentum carried them out into the road where he flicked open his wings and they sped along over the heads of the crowds and the tops of the cars. Then, with a couple of powerful beats, Vicente climbed into the sky as if leaping up a ladder, but with a sensation of slowing at the highest point that gave the impression they might fall out of the sky. Now they were above the buildings with the entire city glowing in the sunshine below.

'Not quite the ending I expected,' Vicente said. 'Are you alright?'

'We did it,' Branca said. 'It may not have been the way I wanted to break the news to my family, but now they know, too. So we may as well get to the honeymoon. The only problem is, we left our luggage behind.'

'Oh, I think we'll manage,' Vicente said as he tilted his head so that he could see Branca. He was smiling.

Branca found herself smiling back. They'd got over the worst. They could sign the register upon their return. For now, she was going to enjoy being with her love as they flapped their leisurely way over the terracotta roofs, across the elegantly cobbled squares, around the square church towers, and down tree-lined boulevards. Towering fluffy white clouds had started to build in the deep blue sky and glowed like monumental wedding cakes.

'We're married now,' Branca whispered.

The future would bring plenty of challenges, but for now she would wallow in her happiness, safe on the wings of her husband.

Marina Pacheco

I am a travelling author who currently lives in Lisbon, after stints in London, Johannesburg, and Bangkok. My ambition is to publish 100 books. It's a challenge I decided upon after I'd completed my 33rd book. Or I should say, my 33rd first draft. I am currently working on getting all of those first drafts into a publishable state. This is taking considerably longer than I'd anticipated! My usual genres are Historical Fiction, Romance ,and Sci-fi/Fantasy.

You can find out more about me and my work, including downloading my free novel, Sanctuary, from my website: https://marinapacheco.me

Iberian Summer Cruise

Nadia Lym

"Sally Margaret Mills! Won't you stop jumping around and please behave?" Mother shouted at me over her fashionable Martini glass, as fashionable as the ensembles that she used to wear. Mother was all about Chanel and Yves Saint-Laurent two-piece suits – and show-stopping evening wear – always in line with the expensive trends of the time and whatever the 35th First-Lady was wearing. It was the start of the glamorous sixties. Jackie O was a fashion icon from the instant she stepped into the White House, and Mother regularly followed her photos in all the glossy magazines.

I adored my parents, adored Mother, but I had the impression that I was not first and foremost in her life.

"Where is your father, now? They said we'll be docking in about fifteen minutes."

I was seven years old in 1962 and my father had convinced Mother to go on an eight-day summer cruise of the Iberian Peninsula, starting in Barcelona. She had quickly agreed to the idea of an "exotic" escape – everything outside the States was exotic to her – no doubt planning to have something different to boast about at her next party.

Aunt Delia and Uncle Fred had already been on this tour and could not stop talking about the wonderful sights. My father had always wanted to visit Europe so he immediately decided to try it.

Mother wanted to leave me behind – at home with Loretta, the help we had then. Luckily, my father insisted that this was also an educational trip for me, assured her that I would be too excited to misbehave, and I was allowed to join them on the vacation. This was a life-changing experience for everyone, in many ways.

I made a lot of new friends on that cruise, most of whom didn't speak English. But kids don't need much to understand each other; I even learned several foreign words; a few swearwords too, much to Mother's displeasure.

It was the morning of our final stop; obeying Mother's instructions, I quit playing hopscotch to look into the distance ahead. This final excursion was already very promising: Lisbon was clearly in sight now, inviting us with its bright orange roofs, multi-coloured façades, and tall green treetops peeking out here and there.

Mother turned her round, oversized sunglasses towards my father, who had just arrived at her side: "There you are, Marvin, dearest!" she said to him. "Do you think it will be hot in Lisbon? I don't want to catch too much sun on the excursion. Gibraltar was impossibly hot, and Seville was an extension of this. I hope the food here is better. Are we going to walk all the time again? I don't want to get tired."

"Delia said that Lisbon is quite charming," my father said with his warm enthusiasm, "that the locals are friendly, and the fish is so fresh and tasty. They have tramcars here, just like in Chicago. Wouldn't you girls love to ride in one? And we can always take a cab, Arlena, if we need to. We'll have a great time, girls!"

Mother merely pursed her lips. A minute later she was returning to the cabin to "touch up" her make-up. She returned wearing a stylish hat and the emerald necklace that my father had recently given her to mark their tenth wedding anniversary – a costly replica of one worn at a White House gala.

"Do you have to wear that necklace on the excursion?"

"Why, Marvin, we *have* to make a good impression," she dismissed him.

"On whom?" my father countered, not really wishing to start an argument.

Moments later we were docking at Lisbon harbour. Mother walked proud and triumphant in her Chanel and Tiffany creations, faultless, from the carefully coiffed hair to the nail polish matching the colour of her outfit. My father held on to my hand and together we followed the other passengers ashore. As we walked toward the meeting point, I imagined us to be intrepid explorers, ready to discover the secrets of Lisbon, armed with our little baskets, and colourful hats and head-scarves.

Having received information on the time passengers were expected to meet back there in order to return to the ship, each family or couple went on their separate sightseeing tour.

The travel agency had assigned us a tour guide: Manuel. He joined us at the meeting point and escorted us along the streets of Lisbon. Due to the time constraint, we were going to focus on the more historical sights. I could barely contain my excitement.

Most of the time we walked along pavements made out of small black and white blocks of stone – mosaics, really – arranged in original patterns and designs. The sky was so blue! Our Manhattan skies were grey compared to this. And the light? Lisbon's light was so unique! I remember so well how it had a gold, bright, warm quality to it that never in my life have I found anywhere else, in spite of my many travels. I miss that light, and I confess that I miss those fleeting, almost perfect family moments.

I listened with interest while Manuel explained all about the history of Lisbon. We started at the *Praça do Comércio* (or Commerce Square), observing the U-shaped construction and galleries that surround it. This replaced the Royal Palace that was swept away by the large earthquake and giant wave that destroyed part of the city in the eighteenth century, and was designed as the new commercial hub of Lisbon. It was part of the rebuild effort led by Portugal's then Prime Minister, a powerful Marquis with big plans, both architectural and political. I didn't grasp all the meanings of Manuel's comments, back then, but I imagined this larger-than-life, evil conspirator, plotting the streets of Lisbon.

Lisbon is built on seven hills, just like Rome. We walked awhile then took a tram-car to see the remains of St. George's Castle. There was a steep incline to cover from the last stop to the castle entrance. I let go of my father's hand and beat them all there.

Mother had sacrificed comfort for elegance; her high-heel shoes did not agree with the gradient and she started complaining to my father. He listened patiently and gently suggested that she might walk the last stretch barefoot. She reacted with horror and haughtily carried on. In spite of everything, she still looked amazing. She always dazzled everyone with her ability to look splendid in any situation, from dusk till dawn.

We took the opportunity to sit down, rest a little, drink, and eat a sandwich. Manuel went on to point out the five main viewpoints in Lisbon that we could see from there, and how each of these in turn also allowed us to admire this and the other four sites. The view from the Castle was indeed commanding. I was enchanted by the cityscape, my eyes forever drawn to the blue horizon, where the river merges with the sky.

We left St. George's Castle and went down to explore the heart of the oldest part of town just below it: the old medieval Moorish quarter called Alfama. I noticed how the narrow winding roads there were a clear contrast to the clean, straight lines of the broad thoroughfares I had seen in the part closer to the river, the one rebuilt by the evil Marquis.

We stopped at a traditional restaurant to have lunch. Our meal consisted of a mouth-watering dish of rice mixed with different kinds of seafood, which my father loved and Mother ate because she was hungry. All the while she made sure to point out how her own home cooking was better (although she never actually prepared it herself. My parents employed a wonderful lady called Ana-Mae, who was a chef at heart; she cooked all our tasty meals, sometimes with Loretta's help).

My father listened patiently, occasionally adding a "*Yes, dear!*" and winking at me. We both knew what she was like. He loved her all the same, and always forgave her small superficialities. And paid her bills. I still recall a magnificent evening gown that must have cost a fortune: off one shoulder, made of light-yellow silk with an overlay of crepe chiffon and matching sash. She looked splendid in it. She did possess something that could be described as innately charming.

My father held on to my hand and made sure that I was having fun, that I was not tired or hungry, or in need of anything.

Our tour continued in Alfama. I noticed again those interesting, colourful tiles, which reminded me of the ones I had seen in Seville. The locals, especially in Portugal, used these as decorative features in almost any construction, especially for façades. In some cases, they were even used to tell stories with pictures; small pieces of a puzzle coming together on a large panel to illustrate ancient battles, seafaring conquests, or even the lives of Saints. I thought of these as comic books before the invention of comic books.

As the afternoon slowly progressed towards the end, so did our tour; we were now heading back to the meeting point.

It was at this moment that we were startled by two sinister-looking individuals who snatched me from my father's grasp and threatened me at knife point, demanding, in exchange for my life, that my parents give up all their valuables.

My father immediately offered all the money in his wallet plus his wrist-watch, pleading for my safety. But their eyes were inevitably drawn to Mother's ostentatious adornment; they only wanted this.

"No, not my necklace!" Mother cried.

I was terrified but I still recorded everything in my mind. Years later I had the time and maturity to reflect upon those events, and again as I narrate them here: my father's desperation; Mother's hand protecting her precious replica of the Tiffany creation. It was the first time I had seen her this vulnerable.

"Arlena," my father entreated, "give them the necklace!"

"But, but... perhaps we can offer something else! *Tell*

them, Manuel," she shouted to our guide.

My father stared in shock.

"Arlena!" he cried in angry disbelief. "Do you value that necklace more than your own daughter?"

"But... but it's..." she tried to say, yet she knew that it was pointless and misplaced. Reluctantly, she unclasped the jewellery and gave it to my father.

The necklace was exchanged for my safety, the criminals disappeared, and I was gladly returned to my father's arms.

Manuel couldn't stop apologising; Arlena couldn't stop wailing after the loss of her precious necklace. The pride of her beauty, her vain success, all shattered in one moment. What would have happened if she had never worn it? If she had never had to choose? How strange life is, how capricious! How little is needed to ruin or save; or to expose your weaknesses.

They went to the nearest police station, but there was little the police could do apart from collecting all the information and issuing a report.

My father never forgave Mother; he pointed out that she had decided to wear the jewelry in spite of his warning, and this sealed the matter. My parents' marriage was never the same after this. The spell was broken. They eventually divorced, a matter of months after our return home.

I went to live with my aunt and uncle for some time, while my father sorted out his life, and Mother... well, Arlena never even fought for custody of me. She chose to leave. And after she moved out, we never heard from her again.

My father remarried and I went to live with him again. Joan, his new wife, was more a mother to me than Arlena had ever tried to be. We have been to Europe many times again since. But these are other narratives; perhaps I might tell them one day.

The purchase or loss of a necklace has influenced the lives of a few famous characters, it seems. Fact or fiction, some books recount these. This was *my* story.

Nadia Lym

I love travelling. This has led me to visit and live in different places before moving back to Portugal. Likewise, a journey to the past is a fascinating adventure for me. For this reason, I enjoy writing historical fiction, mainly focusing on Early Nineteenth Century England.

At the end of 2020, after several years in the works, I finally brought a stack of scattered pages together into a cohesive narrative, proudly giving life to a dream: I completed and revised the initial draft of my first novel, *Light and Darkness*. And while that one is resting, like a fine wine before it is ready to be tasted, I am writing the next installment of my characters' adventures. Stay tuned!

Lisbon Blues

Nuno Neves

They met at Estufa Fria, the Cold Greenhouse, in the midst of the water droplets floating in air. Two very similar men, one generation apart.

"Hi, dad," said Henrique, without taking his hands from the pockets.

Marco opened his arms to closely embrace his son, not saying a word. They stood motionless for more than one minute. In spite of the cold, Henrique started sweating due to the warmth generated with such contact. He finally took his hands out and responded to the hug. There were tears on his neck.

"What's happening?"

Halting the clench, Marco gazed at Henrique's eyes, until both had the same stare.

They started walking, slowly perambulating the entire gallery and inhaling the scent of the plants. Their gestures seemed coordinated, somehow determined by a genealogical choreography. And so they went from the artificial dampness of the greenhouse to the chilling haze of the winter outside.

Always leading, Marco chose the path to the parking lot, an endless ramp of slippery asphalt they started to climb. Tourist buses were arriving, releasing Britons in shorts and t-shirts as if it was a Summer day. They would probably take a stroll on Parque Eduardo VII after visiting the greenhouse. According to some reports, it was tourists by day and homosexual mating by night in that park. It was said about a renowned politician that he was a predator there. He had become Minister of Defense.

The climb eventually took them, after a right turn, to the belvedere with the Portuguese flag and a marble fountain of the Portuguese sculptor João Cutileiro that resembled a penis. Sometimes Henrique wondered if the Botero fountain in Campo Grande of a large woman expelling water from her nipples belonged to the same project.

Beside the marble penis, which would be surrounded by tourists in a short while, they stared at the splendor of the Tagus river, bordering the city. Pompous and green, on the top of a column of white stone, the bronze statues of Marquês de Pombal and a walking lion turned their bottoms to them, making sure all would understood the importance of assholes to the nation. The marble penis kept ejaculating gallons of water. A huge container ship moved towards the marquis to behead him.

Henrique was tempted to share such wisecracks with his father, to lighten the mood, but he knew beforehand it wasn't a good idea. The head of the *Marquis of Dovecot* disappeared against the dark hull of the passing container ship, an optic decapitation of the anti-Semitic reconstructor of Lisbon.

"Ha-ha!" To Henrique's astonishment, Marco was pointing at the statue and bursting with laughter, as if he himself was the pilot of the vessel. His eyes were fixed, wide open, and ice cold. He kept pointing dutifully, his laugh a replacement for words.

He turned back all of a sudden to cross the road. Drivers stopped and their eyes followed him by the large crosswalk. A faithful servant, Henrique saluted them politely, his teeth attempting to announce the wonders of some televised toothpaste. Not even on purpose, father and son stopped by the water mirror. Their flickering bodies flew by the gray sky, barely distinguished from each other.

"They're going to build the damn thing." Marco let the tip of his shoes touch the water on the gray cobblestones. He bowed his chest and opened the arms again, this time to mimic an albatross. "I am so naive."

"Dad..."

"Seriously, Son. I believed I could stop them."

"So did I."

"No, you didn't." Tilting his wings, Marco glided left and right. "You made a marvelous effort to believe with me, but your instinct is pretty smart. I should have followed it. Your instinct."

"What did they say about your project?"

"It's wonderful. An excellent and innovative piece of architecture and engineering. Very beautiful and functional, but they can't build it."

"Too expensive?"

"Nope. Much cheaper."

"What was their excuse, then?

Marco turned the palm of is hands to the sky and smiled.

"This time they were quite creative."

"Tell me. What line did they use to choose building that eyesore instead of your project?"

"Ready?"

"Come on, Dad!"

Facing his reflection, Marco closed his arms.

"I am not famous enough." He laughed as an evil genius, hiding each blow of ax lacerating his heart. "Ah-ah! Straight to the mass grave of the Brotherhood of Non-Sodomized Architects! Let's get ourselves drunk and sing some fado, brothers! Let's cry out our miseries as thousands of other creative souls horrified with the prospect of oblivion. Feed your egos with sourness and go meditate."

The reflection of Henrique turned to his father's eyes.

"Is that your choice?"

Another laugh.

"Now, *you*'re being naive." They faced each other, both beings and images. "There is no choice. This is destiny. I am one of thousands condemned to obscurity and, worse than everything, never with the chance of working on their ideas. Our creative lives are amputated." Another monstrous laugh. "What else could I expect? This is Portugal. This is Lisbon."

Henrique recalled the famous quotation from Portuguese writer Eça de Queirós:

"Portugal is Lisbon. The rest is landscape."

"What landscape?" cried Marco. "We're screwing up far beyond the horizon. Look at the farting castle. Locals are being forced to leave so that tourists have their romantic vacations among the stench of rotten sardines and foreign billionaires invest in real estate while promoting their business with the *saudade* bullshit. Don't people know grammar anymore? Portuguese use a noun instead of a verb to express how they miss someone. It's as simple as that. No need to speculate around semantics. This is form, plain and simple. Morphology. Syntax. Noun, verb. Tadaaaaah!..." Arms wide open once more to perform a short dervish spiral. "Ages of perpetuating baloney, like the statue in Rossio. The body of Emperor Maximiliano, of Mexico, and the head of Pedro IV, of Portugal. Truth or urban legend, who cares? This is us. All appearances, kitsch forms on dubious content from the deep souls of grocers." The soles of Marco's shoes were all in water now. "Do you want a career? Be friends with the local grocer. Spread open your buttocks and get in to tribal mode. To the Palace of Justice!" he shouted.

While bordering the Amalia Rodrigues garden, Marco started singing his own *fado à desgarrada*, shaking both head and shoulders as one solid piece:

Oh, beaaauuuutifuuul Lisboooon,
of grooooocers and bruuutes,
who gave me the leeeessoooon
to sell of my guuuuts.

In spite of his efforts, Henrique wasn't capable of calming his father down. He sang, spiraled and glided towards the pedestrian overpass on Marquês de Fronteira street. There was no shortage of marquis in Lisbon.

"Can't you adapt your project to somewhere else, Dad?"

Marco flew in circles around his son.

"You know me better. I can start from zero any time. I like zero. Only zero is receptive to context. Architecture is harmony with context. No grocer's greedy adaptation to capitalize kitsch.

"Sorry. My bad."

"Glad to know I still have nonsense for you to learn from." Smiling as a naughty lad, Marco dived his airplane in to the overpass. "Here I go, the Japanese Zero Kamikaze! Banzaaaaai!..." His feet stamped the wooden floor, leaving the wet mark of his soles, a trail to fast disappear on the damp Monsanto Bridge. The suicidal voyage of some forgotten architect.

No way Henrique would let his father move from him. They flew over the traffic jam as a squadron of zealous guardians of the skies. The Palace of Justice waited for them on the other side. Lisbon penitentiary was a few meters on their left. Marco stopped and placed the prison building on a rectangle made with his thumbs and index fingers. Henrique peeked at the composition.

"Are you considering a project for criminals?" he asked.

"All projects are for criminals nowadays. They're commissioned by criminals, conceived by criminals, and capitalized by criminals. This is called high finance, the engine of economies."

Henrique slowly landed one hand on his father's shoulder.

"Those are the ways since the dawn of time, everywhere. You would still be a victim in any other city in the world."

"Is it my fault, then? Am I alienated? Is decency and competence nothing but wishful thinking?"

"Sometimes things turn out OK."

"Not in this country and certainly not in this city." Closing one eye, Marco peered acutely through the rectangle, now on vertical. "This prison needs expanding to the clouds."

"Would you ever build a prison?"

"I better not. I would be concerned about the well-being of the prisoners. These real estate criminals do not deserve the accommodations of my projects."

Now it was Henrique's turn to laugh.

"So, them refusing you is good news."

They both laughed like crazy, hoping to dissolve their despair on the acid of awareness. The path continued on the backside of the building along a bike lane. The hidden balance. A dark shadow was cast on them by the Palace of Justice. The journey waiting them wouldn't be a bright one, no matter how enlightened they were.

Those were the ways of life. That was Lisbon blues.

Saturday, August 7th 2021

Nuno Neves

Nuno Neves was born in Évora in 1976 and lives in Odivelas, near Lisbon. He is the author of the science fiction novel *O Sentido Latente*, published in 2003 by Editorial Presença, and the trilogy of witty essays *Beyond the Belly Button*, available on Amazon, with the titles: *Fifty Life Lessons: How to face life as it really is!*; *A Male's Love Pursuit: A portrait of a man's subconscious mind seeking for affection*; and *Oh, My God!: A few words on faith and scepticism.* Nowadays, he is working on the graphic novel *Chronos*, publishing its panels on the site Nuno Neves Store while they're being drawn. He also writes compositions of electronic music, distributed on YouTube, Spotify, iTunes and several other platforms.

https://nunonevesstore.com/

Dream Destination

Phil Town

I would like it to be sunny there. Sun gives you vitamin ... some-letter-or-other. But not too much, eh? Some sun — good; too much — bad! Wear a hat. Sunglasses. Factor some-high-number sun block. But yes, sun. Apart from the vitamin intake, there's the sense of well-being. Apparently, the further north you are, like here, where skies are grey, days shorter, rain aplenty, the suicide rate is appalling. I'm not ready to go yet. Give me sunshine.

I would like it to have people, naturally. I'm fond of people. No, really. I mean, they're okay. Depending. I'd rather not meet too many of my compatriots there, though — at least not the ones who think pouring whole barrels of beer down their gullets then consigning it to the gutter soon afterwards, from either end, is their idea of cultural exchange. Local people — friendly, welcoming, with an exotic language I can't understand and sometimes we have to use gestures to communicate and that makes us laugh and get on like a house on fire. That kind of people.

I would like it to have a cuisine. Nothing too fancy, mind you. As long as it's better than old Mrs Wilson's efforts, like this evening's bangers and mash; I'm still chewing a piece of one of her sausages three hours later! It doesn't have to be Michelin five-star gourmet, the cuisine — you know, a flake of fish, a spud, a sprig of parsley and a special sauce trickled into an artistic design on the side of the plate; I'm a simple bloke, with simple tastes. But there has to be something typical you can get your teeth into, and not just stuff you can find on any high street from Wales to New South Wales and all points east and west. Some fresh sardines, for instance, charcoal-grilled, with roast peppers on the side. That kind of thing. Lovely!

I would like it to have forms of transport that set it apart. A funicular maybe, which costs you a couple of quid for a two-minute climb you could have walked, but that's okay because it's different. Old trams, too — the somehow-comforting clunk-clank-clunk of iron wheels on iron tracks, and the dull bell to get people out of the way, and all the locals moaning when some idiot parks on the tracks and we have to wait while he comes out of the shop and raises an apologetic hand and we all swear at him in our different languages. And spotting the pickpockets and warning fellow travellers, but getting dirty, threatening looks from the thieves because you've ruined their business, until the next tram they catch. But it's worth the danger because you feel a bit of a hero. Me, a hero? Yes, why not?

I would like it to have interesting things to see, of course. A river with docks and iconic bridges maybe. A castle on top of a hill. A wide, tree-lined avenue, where people promenade of a Sunday. Museums with local art, and maybe some international stuff, too — I don't know, the odd Picasso wouldn't go amiss. And views over the city — nothing like a belvedere to take in the exquisite higgledy-piggeldyness of terracotta rooftops, baking in the sun.

I would like it to be old, my destination, at least in parts. Not just the same dusty cathedrals and bits of Roman wall, long since collapsed and little more than rubble now. No, I mean old and decaying. There's a certain beauty in decay, in crumbling masonry, flaky paintwork, half-rotting doors. I wouldn't want to spend my life surrounded by mould and grime and cockroaches, mind you (I spent three weeks in the east wing, and that was enough). But passing through, and from a safe distance ... yes, decay beats modern any day.

I would like it to have quiet squares. You've been walking all day, seeing the sights, and you get off the main street and into a bit of shade, and at the end of the side street you see a sunny space, and you walk towards it, and it opens up into a lovely little square, with maybe fragrant jacaranda trees in bloom and a quaint kiosk selling coffee. You buy one — a tiny cup, very bitter, that you don't really like but when in Rome ... even though you're not actually in Rome — and you sit on the terrace, sip your coffee, grimace, take out your book, read a few pages in between watching the world pass sedately by.

I would like it to be a place where I could fall in love, even if it's a Mr-Bernstein-from-Citizen-Kane kind of love. An elegant young woman dressed in white (white parasol optional), possibly drifting past the terrace where I'm sitting, and she doesn't see me, but there's not a week goes by after that day that I don't think of her. And years later I'm still thinking of her, and still in stupid, impossible, unrequited love.

I would like to dream of her tonight. That would be a nice dream. Beauty and warmth together, like my destination. Until I wake up, and I'm still here.

Well, maybe that's a good point to end. Miller's been looking daggers at me for ages; he wants to use the pen and I *have* been hogging it a bit. But this should be enough for us to go on in the next session, Doctor Moletta, don't you think?

And anyway, it'll be lights-out soon.

*A version of this story was first published in the online literary magazine **Short Fiction Break**.*

O Senhor do Adeus

Phil Town

You have a happy childhood, spent largely in the bosom of your family. Your father is a diplomat and takes you and your mother with him around the world. You see sights that few so young might have the chance to see. But the friends you make along the way are left behind as the family moves to yet another city. And another.

Like homing pigeons, you all return to Lisbon eventually, when your father retires. Then he passes and you are left, you and your mother, to look after each other. You travel together and grow closer and closer; there is no love like that of a mother's.

Then your mother passes too. It is inevitable. It is life. But you are not ready. You have not prepared yourself for the aching solitude – those interminable nights in silent rooms that echo with memories of happier times.

You flee into the city streets. The noise and bustle are a balm to your grieving soul. You pass young couples embracing, older couples strolling in familiar comfort. But you? You have no one. No one that close. Not anymore.

You come to a stop, alone in the night, conspicuous in your elegant overcoat and scarf, at one of the city's busiest points, with its streams of cars and buses full of those returning home, or on their expectant way to meetings with friends and loved ones, perhaps.

Someone honks their horn at you as their car passes. You wave, instinctively. They wave back. You smile to yourself; it is human contact of sorts. You stand for several minutes, contemplating a return to the crushing emptiness of your apartment. Then another honk of a horn, another exchange of waves.

You take the initiative and wave at the next car that passes. This time there is no recognition. You try again. Nothing. Again. And again. And then there it is: a young woman waves back. You try again. Nothing. Then nothing. Then nothing. Then a wave.

The force of the waves easily trumps the disappointment of the nothings. You continue deep into the evening, until the tiredness sets in; you are not young anymore. You return to the apartment. It is still cavernously empty, but now you can bear it a little better because inside you there is a glow.

And the glow takes you out the next evening to the same spot, to do the same. Tonight, you set about your task with more enthusiasm, and it bears fruit. People do not always respond, but they respond more often than yesterday. You enjoy the reactions – the waves and the honking of horns.

You are oblivious to the likely observations of those in the passing cars: that you may not be entirely of sound mind. But even if you knew, you would not care. Because you are making connections, with strangers, and they are already becoming your lifeblood.

You soon become a human landmark in the city. People go out of their way to wave and honk. They call you *O Senhor do Adeus*. You prefer *O Senhor do Olá*, but it never sticks. For ten long years the joy you get from these strangers drives away that "evil lady" solitude (your words), but you know that you also give joy back.

You make several close friends through your new vocation. Every Sunday you go to the cinema with two of them, and you write reviews that are published online. The last one you write is about the film *The Social Network*. In the last lines, you hope "that everyone will be very happy."

Soon after, on a cold night in November, the car horns are silent, people's waves left unwaved. A friend lays a bouquet of lilacs at your traffic lights. "A person so very alone yet accompanied at the same time by a multitude," she tells the newspapers.

You may like to know that many a tear is shed, and a plaque is placed at your favourite spot – a plaque commemorating a life that made other lives better for so many brief but precious moments.

But a cold, stone plaque is not a warm wave and a smile, is it, *Senhor do Adeus*?

LILOLOLI VOL 1: O SENHOR DO ADEUS

João Manuel Serra, 24 October 1931 — 10 November 2010

Phil Town

Phil Town is a teacher, translator, journalist and writer/screenwriter, based in Lisbon. More of his short stories/flash fiction can be found online at the literary magazine *Short Fiction Break*, and in the Create 50 anthologies *Twisted 50 Vol. Two*, *Twisted's Evil Little Sister*, and *The Singularity*. He also writes about Portuguese football for the British independent football magazine *When Saturday Comes*.

Enjoyed this book?

You can make a huge difference.

If you are like the writers of these stories, you use reviews to decide whether you want to buy a book. So if you enjoyed the book please take a moment to let people know why. The review can be as short as you like.

Thank you very much!

Lightning Source UK Ltd.
Milton Keynes UK
UKHW010643301121
394854UK00001B/215

9 781913 672263